4.—

The Noonday Devil

The Noonday Devil

URSULA CURTISS

DODD, MEAD & COMPANY · NEW YORK

THE NOONDAY DEVIL was serialized under the title
of LOOKING FOR A MAN

Printed in the United States of America
Designed by Stefan Salter

For My Husband
Lt. Col. John Curtiss, U.S.A.R.

The Noonday Devil

OUTSIDE IN THE STREET, with the trailing farewells of the switchboard girls lingering in his ears, Sentry discovered that he was still clutching a tiny crumpled ball of paper in one hand. His left hand; his right had been extended and shaken heartily during the past two hours by every single soul employed in the firm of Ballard and Sergeant, a large percentage of whom were complete strangers.

Rain pelted down at the paper when he smoothed it out. "Memo from the desk of Andrew Sentry;" someone, very probably he himself, had adorned it with a six-legged spider wearing sneakers. Sentry tossed it into the swirling gutter, hoped briefly that it would not be retrieved by his future employers, and began to walk east on Worth Street.

It was at that point that the incalculables began to mesh. His mood, for one thing, the bored, loose-ends, faintly depressed mood of a man who had just wound up four years of work at one job, with no immediate plans ahead. There was the fact that Cy Stevenson couldn't meet him at Tim Costello's until six o'clock and it was now not quite five—and there was the rain, steadily increasing in force and wetness. By the time he had gone three blocks north on Broadway, Sentry had decided abruptly to take shelter in a bourbon old-fashioned.

The bar he turned into was small and dark, with an air of waiting hopefully for the cocktail trade that always went somewhere else. It was, at the moment, nearly deserted. It didn't look at all like the place where destiny, set in motion by the incalculables, would place violent hands on Sentry's life.

He remembered every detail of the bar later with enraging clarity—enraging because so much of it was extraneous, while the tiny simple fact he wanted escaped him in a splinter of time.

He remembered that the bartender who mixed his drink was going off duty and suspended the untying of his apron with great reluctance when Sentry sat down at the bar. A woman's hat hung in his memory, a grotesque image of a baby's bonnet in satin. Opposite its wearer a swarthy man with gold teeth was telling loudly of the eight deer heads he had just had mounted —"mouths open and snarling." Deer—Sentry remembered saying to himself incredulously—snarling?

There was an indeterminate interval of which he recalled only the occasional opening of the door and the gradual increase of background voices, the rain and the blurred oblivious faces beyond the windows. Presently there was a voice with a grin behind it, saying, "Another of the same, Mr. Sentry?"

Sentry looked up, startled. "Mac! Did you come out of the bourbon bottle or have you left Mooney's?"

The barman nodded. "About a month ago. More money—" he winked elaborately "—and less Mooney. Say, how do you like that, Mr. Sentry? I been working on it a month."

Sentry said he thought it was very funny and that Mac should write it down before he forgot it, and that he would have another bourbon. It had just arrived when another voice, this time beside him, said hesitantly, "I beg your pardon . . . he did say Sentry, didn't he?"

Sentry turned, nodding. The man who stood beside him, who was now mounting a stool and putting his half-finished drink on the bar before him, had been sitting alone farther down the

◈ 2

room when Sentry came in. He had a reddened complexion that was either weeks of sun or hours of Scotch, hazel-green eyes that were a little too small under tufted white-gold brows, and a curiously sweet mouth above a deeply-cleft chin. A gray felt hat was cocked carelessly back on his pale head.

He turned an intent gaze on Sentry. "I hope you don't mind my barging in on this, but I couldn't help hearing . . . It's an odd name, Sentry. You don't run across it very often."

Sentry agreed politely that you didn't. After a moment of silence he stopped waiting for a counter-introduction; his visitor had obviously slid past the stage of rituals. He glanced covertly at his watch. It was almost five-thirty. Finish his drink and go; it would take nearly until six to get to Tim Costello's and his appointment with Cy Stevenson at this time of day. He lifted his glass.

"Knew a guy named Sentry once myself." It was idle, companionable. "Long time ago, but not long enough for me, thanks. Army. You in the Army yourself?"

Sentry had put down his glass, so sharply that it jarred his hand. He said, "Air Corps. Italy, most of the time," and stopped on an inquiring note.

"Not you," said the felt-hatted man. "But damned if you're not the dead spit of him. Nice guy, too, hell of a nice guy, he was. Oh well, that's life, I guess, or la guerre or something." He drained his glass and pocketed his cigarettes.

"Wait a minute," said Sentry casually. "What are you drinking?" He caught the bartender's eye, and when the man beside him had ordered a Scotch and water, sat silent a moment, fighting the rise of expectancy. There had undoubtedly been hundreds of men named Sentry in the Army; there was no logic to the sudden tightening of his interest. But it was there, as it had been there, misleadingly, so many times before.

◈ 3

The Scotch and water arrived. The man who had suddenly become the focal point of Sentry's attention lifted his glass, said solemnly, "Hair on your chest," and drank.

Sentry waited until cigarettes had been lit. Then he said idly, looking at the reflected satin bonnet in the bar mirror, "Where did you know this other Sentry?"

The hazel-green eyes flicked at him, flicked away. "Bataan. O'Donnell. Cabanatuan."

And there you have it, thought Sentry. He raised his glass and looked reflectively at the fingers tight around it, and though, Correction: there you've had it. Because the odds against a mistaken identity were lowering now, had lowered almost to nil.

He tried, fragmentarily, another mental approach. It was nearly six years now, six years since half his reason for existence had been sheared away. And the wound that left wouldn't heal until you had stopped opening it, roughly, at every opportunity. If it had been me, he wondered exploringly, and Nick who had gotten the communications from the War Department . . . which solved exactly nothing. It wasn't a question of something owed, or of sensible, long-last acceptance. It wasn't even reasonable, this sense of urgency, because didn't he know all there was to know? Except for the details, which he would have liked to sort out and look at once and shut away forever—and chances were he would never find those. The thought gave Sentry an odd, sober, clear-visioned feeling that might have come from no bourbons or ten. Out of it, he said, "What was this other Sentry's first name?"

The man beside him poked at ice in his drink, frowning, and then looked brightly up at Sentry. "Nick," he said. "Yeah, that's it, Nick Sentry. Captain, Field Artillery." He nodded helpfully at Sentry. "Short for Nicholas, I guess."

◆ 4

It was all short for Nicholas, Sentry thought: the chance meeting in a third-rate bar, his own haphazard stir of attention, the philosophical epitaph uttered by a stranger. Nick had cancelled out into this, and it was still, after six years, bitterly hard to take.

The other man was staring at him curiously. Sentry ordered two more drinks, caught a glimpse of his own too-intent face in the bar mirror and tried to relax. If his inquiries seemed anything more than casual, his informant would close up at once, embarrassed and uneasy, and there would be just another précis of what had happened to Nick. Already there was a question shaping itself in the ruddy face turned toward his. Sentry met it neatly. "Funny how these things go. Just the other day I 'ran across a guy who'd been at O'Donnell."

"You don't say." The Scotch was taking hold. "What was his name?"

"Jorgensen," said Sentry without a flicker.

"Jorgensen. Jorgensen . . . Say, was he a plumber?"

"No." Sentry made it regretful. "As a matter of fact he's a light bulb inspector. In a plant, you know."

"Oh. Then I guess I never . . ." Jorgensen was allowed to go back to limbo. A moment later the detour accomplished what Sentry had hoped it would; the reminiscent look came back to the other man's face. X number of Scotches plus three; Sentry, trying to add it up, thought he was sober enough to keep to the subject, talkative enough to expand on it.

"O'Donnell, Cabanatuan toward the end——" The tufty white-gold brows came together. "In again, out again, gone again Finnegan, that's what it was. Funny how you mean to look up all those guys when you get back . . ." He mentioned names, blurrily, went on into, "Last time I laid eyes on most of them was in January, '45. Come to think of it, it was just a month or

◈ 5

two after poor old Sentry—you remember, the fellow I was telling you about—made his break."

In the mirror behind the bar the woman in the satin baby's bonnet threw back her head and screamed with laughter. A nickelodeon, springing to life somewhere in the back distances, competed with her. Sentry schooled his face, trying to look neither bored nor urgent. He said very carefully, "Made his break?"

The man beside him nodded. "A few weeks more and he could have walked out in style. But you know Sentry—hell, no, you didn't know Sentry, beg your pardon—he never stopped trying. He was cagey, though, he knew they'd take it out on the rest of us if he got caught. He got a plan, finally, and from what I heard later it was a beaut."

A beaut, thought Sentry, expelling his breath gently, but the patient died. He waited.

"It wasn't so much getting out of the place," said the voice close to his ear, "it was how you were going to stay alive once you got into that stinking jungle. Well, there was this Filipino well-digger in camp who was a cousin of a Philippine Scout Sentry had known at Bataan, and I guess the word was passed along for him to look up Sentry. The long and the short of it was that the well-digger was to lead him back into the hills. That was always if, you understand, but there was no if because there was a guard at the fence where there shouldn't have been. That was the whole point of Sentry's plan—that open space. But, brother, it wasn't open that night."

He was drunk now, definitely. But with something in the back of his eyes that wasn't pleasant to look at, that had nothing to do with liquor.

"So they shot him," he said.

"I know," said Sentry.

◆ 6

The greenish eyes, bright and narrowed, swivelled to his. Sentry said without pausing, "They always did, I understand."

"Yes, they did. But I'll tell you another thing. And," said the voice with faint belligerence, "you can ask Twining, or Pavick, or—hell, wait a minute . . ." He fumbled in his breast pocket and brought out a small black notebook. Sentry watched his fingers ruffle unsteadily through the pages. "Here you are."

There were names and addresses in small careful printing on the ruled pages. Sentry only glanced at them, his companion was reading them aloud with slow emphasis, having a little trouble around the consonants. Because of his tenseness, they registered as though they had been sketched in acid in Sentry's sight and hearing. The man beside him closed the notebook and pocketed it again with a shake of the head.

That's that, thought Sentry, suddenly flat, aware that the bourbon was too heavy, that the man was too confidential, that he wanted to get out into the clean sweep of rain again. Well, he knew more now than he had known before, two negatively comforting facts: that "shot while attempting to escape" had not been a pretext for a careless execution; that Nick's try for freedom had been wary and deliberate and not the wild result of an intolerable pressure. What more did he want, what more could there possibly be?

"Tell you another thing"—had the stranger said that before? But not a stranger, because he had seen Nick, talked to Nick long after Sentry had—"because he was a hell of a good guy. Sentry, that I'm telling you about. All right, there's Twining and there's Pavick and Lyons and me, among others, and there's a character who just got into Cabanatuan a week ago, who says his name is Sands. But he doesn't answer to the name of Sands, see, he doesn't turn around quick enough when somebody says,

'Hey, Sands.' So what would you think—granted you haven't got much else to think about?"

"That his name was really Smith or Miller or Archambault." Sentry drained his glass and took out his wallet; he had bled this man of all there was to know and reaction, the sudden slackening of tautened senses, had set in. With the reversal of his interest, boredom descended like a millstone.

"Right," said the man beside him. He was staring into the bottom of his glass as though it contained remembered faces instead of cracked ice; he seemed not to have noticed Sentry's withdrawal. "I told you, didn't I, that there was a guard at the fence where there shouldn't have been a guard. Never was, at that time of night. Now there's Sands, who isn't what he says he is. There's Twining, who heard Sentry talking to someone outside the barracks the night before he pulled off his break. Got that?"

"Got it," said Sentry.

"What somebody ought to get," said the other man reflectively, "is that bastard Sands. My money's on Sands, anyway, because Twining swears that's who Sentry was threatening that night."

He picked up his glass, drained the last drops of ice water, put it down again and said sadly, "You kind of hate to see a guy sold up the river by another American. Particularly to settle a private quarrel. Sentry should have got off into the hills and be walking around like you and me—the odds were a hundred to one. But those Japs with the rifles had been told to expect him."

◈ 8

2

SENTRY stared.

He felt as he had felt once before, after a practice boxing match at college when he had been hit near the heart and for a sickening moment his arms had trailed off into nothingness, his feet had no relation to the canvas they stood on.

The feeling passed, and left only a dull unwillingness. He said experimentally, "That's murder."

"Damn right it was."

"You can't be sure."

"There's no proof, you mean. There's no question about what happened. Hell, what can you do about a thing like that unless you meet up with the guy that did it?"

Shifting images in the bar mirror, a racing chaos in his mind; Sentry turned and looked carefully at the man beside him. Was it his imagination or was the bright green gaze steadier now, the face a little less flushed, the gestures with head and hands more controlled than they had been five minutes ago? The other man might, of course, be drinking himself sober. And the hovering unpleasantness in the back of his eyes earlier might have been just this, the ugly haunting fact he had suddenly needed to tell to someone.

That it was a fact Sentry did not doubt at all. Later, when there was time, he could examine his own stunned acceptance and break it down, if possible, into separate parts of logic. Right now he knew only that he was talking to a man who had lived in prison camp with Nick, who had witnessed the events leading up to his death, and that he must somehow find the answers to a whole new bewildering set of questions.

He tried to brace his mind as he had instinctively braced his body against the shock of what he had heard. He must forget everything, now, but the conversation outside a barracks in the Philippines six years ago, and the man who had called himself Sands.

He began to put questions, careless now of whether he showed too much curiosity. The argument outside the barracks?

"Well, Twining heard that, and the next day, after they'd shot Sentry and a few of us thought the whole thing looked fishy, he told me about it. He's almost sure it was Sands, but it was night and he couldn't see, and inside the barracks it was as black as your hat, so that——"

Sentry interrupted him. "What did Sentry say to this other man, whoever he was?"

"He said——" The man beside him seemed to notice his empty glass for the first time and there was a, to Sentry, maddening interval while he wrestled with his impatience and tried to catch the barman's eye.

The new drink arrived. Sentry, who had barely touched his last, waited grimly. The other man was reflective.

"He said—I remember this part of it—'How long did you think you'd get away with it?' and then something about what he'd do to the other guy when they got back home."

But he didn't get back home, because he couldn't be allowed to. Sentry caught back the feeling of rage that went rocking through his brain. He said, "This—Sands. What was he like?"

"Sands?" Again the pause for reflection, again Sentry's curbed impulse to seize and shake him. "Well, let's see, Sands turned up at Cabanatuan about the end of November, '44 . . ."

He went on talking. Sentry, listening, had the eerie sensation of watching a fadeout on a movie screen, dissolving the yellow-lighted bar, the tangled voices, the crowded mirror, even the cold shell of the drink held tightly in his hand. He was no longer impatient. He was no longer even conscious of himself or of the man beside him; he was watching, with a painfully attentive inner eye, the images that were taking shape around him.

For a short and nightmarish interval, he half became Nick.

Nick Sentry. Aged thirty-two when he died, weighing one hundred and five pounds instead of his former one-eighty. Accustomed by now, after nearly three years of it, to crouching at night in a narrow sliver of darkness that crept with insects. Probably never accustomed to the sounds of dying that echoed now and then through the barracks. Hoarding his energy patiently, warily, because he had a plan.

Sands came into the camp in late November, causing nobody any excitement because he was just another ragged, half-starved prisoner. He kept pretty much to himself, as much as you could in a ten-by-twenty barracks with twelve men in it, but among the few men who paid any attention to him there was a general impression that his name was not Sands. There wasn't much to go on, except that he had to be spoken to twice before he'd turn around. And he wasn't deaf. There was just something—funny —about Sands.

He was a man of about thirty, give or take a few years. He had a moustache—but so did a lot of prisoners who had never worn one before and never would again but were baffled by the shaving problem. He was of average height, and dark-haired. He had a funny way of laughing, not that there was much laughing done; sharp and sudden, either long before or long after the point of general amusement.

◈ *11*

Nobody had thought much about Sands one way or another until after the night of December tenth. On the preceding evening he had traded his ration of rice for two cigarettes, and it was probable that he had slipped outside the barracks for a few precious puffs. He would have been beaten if he'd been caught, but you got used to weighing that up and deciding soberly which you'd prefer. Nick had been standing guard that night, and Nick followed him out.

And Twining, First Lieutenant Robert, heard the brief and whispered interchange. Nick: "How long did you think you'd get away with it?" And an inaudible response. Then the mention of something or other being done when they got back to the States—the words that had cost Nick his life.

Twining, thought Sentry, emerging slowly from the half-world. *Twining*. The address was still etched in his memory: Dip Street, Chicago.

Light and sound came back, and the red reflective face of the man beside him. "I'd like to meet Mr. Sands," said Sentry, speaking slowly. "In fact, I'd go a long way to meet Mr. Sands."

The other man shrugged and drained his glass. "What can you do? He did his damage and it's six years ago, he may be in Spanish Morocco by now. Anyway, what——"

"Nick Sentry was my brother," Sentry told him, and found a savage pleasure in it.

"Your bro—— Your what? For God's sake, why didn't you say something? I wouldn't've . . . Good God." His companion wriggled miserably on the bar stool. Gradually his eyes, too green, too small, circled back to Sentry's face and stayed there, wide with uneasiness.

Sentry wasn't looking at him. He was watching the reflected face of a woman directly behind him who, apparently unaware of the telltale qualities of a mirror, was grimacing down at the back of his head and nodding violent encouragement to the lone woman in the booth she had just left. She caught his eye, assumed a face of concrete, turned away and called back to the booth, "I really must run, the Tobeys will be waiting. Bye-bye, dear." She bumped confusedly into a man just entering, righted herself and fled.

Cy Stevenson . . . Good Lord. The woman's haste reminded Sentry of his forgotten appointment, and he was startled into saying the words aloud. He glanced at his watch and turned to the still-staring man beside him.

"Mind ordering another for us? I've got a phone call, won't take a minute."

The bar was fairly crowded now. Sentry maneuvered his way to the phone booth, conscious of something very like exultation. *Twining,* said his brain; *Pavick, Lyons.* While he waited for the number at Tim's to ring, he fished an envelope from his pocket, steadied it against the wall and wrote down the addresses as he remembered them.

There was an inquiring voice in his ear. Sentry asked it if Mr. Stevenson was around, and thought, There are other names, other addresses, and then detached himself with difficulty.

"Cy? . . . Sentry."

"Andrew, my boy." The hollow sound of another phone booth with muffled merriment outside it. "I've been waiting for you ever since three martinis and one lost bet. Where the hell were you when the clock struck six?"

"Sorry," said Sentry, uncontrite. "Cy, I've run into a guy——"

"I see. Give her our regards, will you?"

"—who was in prison camp with Nick."

Cy Stevenson's voice changed, became awkward with concern. "Hey, if you're looking for a reason to tie one on, you've got it already, remember? This is the day you removed your august presence from Ballard and Sergeant. I thought we were really going to wrap that up."

"We will." Although the booth wasn't hot Sentry could feel dampness springing out along his forehead. "Look, Cy, this guy has a lot to tell me."

More arguments at the other end of the wire; Sentry was free at last after promising to join Cy later in case he changed his mind.

He reached the bar and found out that it had been changed for him.

Where he and the gold-eyebrowed man had sat were two vacant bar stools. A fresh bourbon waited at Sentry's place, with an emptied glass beside it.

Sentry paused blankly, meeting a new wave of implication. It flashed across his mind that the absence might be temporary—but the drained glass was eloquently final. He was not surprised when a man next to him turned his head and said affably, "Your friend had to leave. I guess he remembered something in a hurry."

"Oh, I see. Thanks. Didn't leave a message, did he?"

"Nope. Might have had one too many, though," said his informant critically. "He looked a little green around the gills."

A little green around the gills . . . Sentry thanked him again, got his check, nodded mechanically to something the barman said, and made his way out to the street.

Rain met him, and a swimmy strip of wet-night color, neon red and green and orange tangled in black satin streets. Sentry stood just outside the doorway of the bar, trying to orient himself in the rushing, plunging light. Between him and the flow of traffic north on Canal Street were hurrying shapes that gradually identified themselves as three French sailors and a solitary woman with an umbrella. To the south a very old man, overcoated to his heels, felt his way uncertainly along the sidewalk. The opposite side of Broadway was, for the moment, empty of pedestrians.

Sentry hesitated briefly and then swung back into the bar. Mac was pouring whisky sours. He glanced up, caught Sentry's eye, nodded, carried the whisky sours to the far end of the room and came back. In answer to Sentry's quiet question he shook his head slowly. He knew nothing of the gold-eyebrowed man beyond the fact that he had come in three or four times during the past month, at about five o'clock. He was always alone and always took one more than the law required. "But very quiet about it, very," said Mac judiciously. "I figure he works somewhere around here and has troubles. Tonight's the first time I ever see him talk to anybody, though. Usually he just comes in and kind of broods."

Sentry thanked him and went out into the rainy darkness again. No loose ends there. He began to walk north, feeling light-headed. He was getting it now, the full impact of what he had heard half an hour ago. Nick hadn't been just one more casualty of war. Nick had died because another man wanted him to die, for his own secret and desperate reasons.

Murder—cloaked under wartime circumstance, carried out in a Japanese prison camp, announced crisply by the War Department. A neat job, a hellishly neat job, because other fingers had pulled the trigger and those were the rules of war.

Nick, murdered. And the news of his death killing Christopher Sentry, who didn't live to see his elder son's posthumous citation.

My God, thought Sentry, feeling it like a steady probe just under the ribs. Someone had known or overheard Nick's plan for escape from Cabanatuan. Someone who had then gone coolly and thoughtfully to the nearest guard and been taken probably to a higher echelon to tell his story there, so that there would be no possible chance of Nicholas Sentry's survival.

Sentry crossed Canal Street against the lights and found himself beside a disgorging taxi. A plump man who had been holding a furled umbrella austerely aloft started forward. Sentry slid into the cab, told the driver "Uptown," and began to concentrate.

The man in the bar had talked too freely, that much was obvious. He had reached the talkative stage by the time Sentry came in, and the barman's identification, the usage of the familiar name, had further joggled his tongue. Later, when he realized Sentry's connection with the man who he had sworn was murdered, he had become—what?

Sentry lighted a cigarette in the fleeing darkness of the cab and tried to pin down the expression in the widened hazel-green eyes. It hadn't been only agonized embarrassment at having told the dead man's brother the details of his murder, nor the fear that would have come from any kind of complicity.

Wariness. They were at Washington Square before the word sprang into Sentry's mind and fitted perfectly there, explaining the stare, the tiny withdrawal, the swift disappearance of the man in the bar. He had known there would be questions and more questions, and possibly an official inquiry—and he definitely wasn't having any. This in spite of the fact that he had volunteered the story, had told it almost with eagerness, as though he were dislodging an ugly but half-forgotten weight.

The cab driver paused for a light at Eighth Street. He said indifferently over his shoulder, "Uptown's a long way, Mister. Any particular place you got in mind?" and shifted gears with a fracturing sound.

Sentry hesitated. The taxi had begun to move, was past Tenth Street when he said suddenly, "Let me out at the corner of Eleventh, will you?"

Sarah Devany, who had been Nick's fiancée, lived somewhere on Eleventh Street. Sentry had long since forgotten the address, but he would know the doorway of her apartment building when he saw it. He would always know that particular doorway.

Wasn't it possible that there might be some clue, some mention of Sands by that or another name, in Nick's letters to Sarah before he had been captured? Or—Sentry's steps quickened as he remembered it—in the prescribed postcard from prison camp that had reached her only a day or two before the news of his death?

If there were anything, a name or a key to a name, it would be there.

Cursing the rain, the obscuring darkness and his own lack of memory, Sentry moved exploringly west on Eleventh Street, stopping at intervals to stare into lobbies with an intensity that made a very large man with a very small dog turn and eye him suspiciously. A flight of brownstone steps going up, a chaste sign announcing a dentist within, a building with window-boxes full of pale flowers blotting upwards to the rain . . . there it was.

Three marble steps descending from the street, flanked by curving black iron grillwork; Sentry didn't need to glance at the number above the doorway. He knew this place, knew it with a savage hostility that hadn't dimmed in six years. Now, opening the gilt-scrolled outer door, putting a finger mechanically on the bottom right-hand button, he could feel the remembered anger pounding at his temples again.

An answering buzzer sounded. Sentry opened the inner door under its waspish summons, and rang the bell of Apartment 1A.

3

'I HE SILENCE in the little hallway seemed tomblike. No echo of a
stir inside the apartment, no approaching footsteps; suppose,
Sentry inquired shakenly of himself, she has married and moved
away? But no, not married; he had seen Sarah at a large and
confused cocktail party a few weeks ago, and he was almost sure
he would have noticed a ring. There hadn't been one . . . had
there?

The door of 1A swung inward suddenly, surprising Sentry
with his finger poised in mid-air, halfway to the bell. A girl with
pale shining hair cut like a child's stood regarding him out of
enormous dark blue eyes. She was in evening dress, something
slender and white with a wink of gold at one shoulder. She said
briskly, "Oh, I'm so sorry," and began to close the door in Sentry's face.

"Wait a minute," began Sentry to the cream-colored panels.
His imperative tone caught the door just before it closed. "Is
Sarah—is Miss Devany in?"

The door reversed itself and Sentry, with a depth of relief,
heard the girl say, "I am sorry. I thought as a matter of fact you
were Sarah. When she knows I'm in she doesn't bother to dig
for her key. If you're a friend of hers, won't you come in and
wait? She's due any minute . . ."

In the living room just beyond the tiny foyer Sentry introduced himself, and thought there was a look of recognition in
the huge solemn eyes. "How do you do, Mr. Sentry. I'm Sarah's
cousin Megan—Megan Ware. She's very angelically put me up
here for the past two months."

"I know I've heard her speak of you," said Sentry falsely.

"I'm going out myself," said Miss Ware apologetically, and put her hands to her shoulders in a naïve and charming gesture. "I'm only half-dressed. I know Sarah won't be long, so if you'll excuse me . . ."

Half-dressed meant perfume to come, probably. When she had disappeared through a doorway at the far end of the room, Sentry began to walk about, trying to control his braced, patrolling stride. He stopped once to look around him, and the small portion of his mind that was not concerned with the immediacy of his errand noted that the room was changed. What he recalled as a gay and unworried tossing-together of color was now severely white and gray and the bloomy blue-purple of Concord grapes. Under a small and probably valuable etching were tulips like a small red explosion amid the general restraint.

The letters, the post-card. Chances were that she hadn't kept them, but she might remember . . . Sentry went on pacing restlessly back and forth in Sarah Devany's oddly sober living room.

There were infinitesimal sounds from the bedroom beyond: the glassy click of a perfume stopper, a jostling of coat hangers, the light progress of sandalled feet. Megan Ware appeared in the doorway and smiled at Sentry a little anxiously just as the street buzzer broke the waiting silence.

The girl was obviously relieved; she hadn't, Sentry realized, known quite what to do with him. Whether the newcomer were her escort or Sarah Devany, it would be someone to shoulder the responsibility now standing inexorably in front of Sarah's fireplace.

She opened the apartment door, murmuring an apology to Sentry, and stepped out into the hall, drawing the door nearly closed behind her. Her voice floated clearly in: "Darling. Isn't

◈ *19*

it a foul night? But I don't suppose it will be raining in the Plaza."

There were more murmurs, easily translatable as a plea to the man to cope somehow with the dubious situation inside. Then the door swung open and Megan came back in, followed by a man in evening clothes. She said gayly, "Mr. Sentry, Mr. Farrar. Mr. Sentry is a friend of Sarah's, Charles."

The two men stepped forward to shake hands, Sentry returning to his tactical position on the hearth.

Farrar wasn't handsome, but he had the scrubbed impeccable look that would probably confuse a great many people into thinking he was. He appeared to be in his mid-thirties, with the kind of firm-cheeked boyishness that indicated he would look exactly the same ten years hence. There was something almost unnatural about his gleaming cleanliness; to Sentry he bore the air of having been carved out of soap, nicely tinted, and set up as a convincing dummy for Mr. Farrar who was unfortunately unable to be present.

He had known Nick, Sentry was almost sure of that. Because while Megan Ware had shown a stir of recognition at his name, and had undoubtedly known its connection with her cousin, Farrar's face had been shocked fleetingly by Sentry's resemblance to the man Sarah Devany was to have married.

In fact, Farrar seemed about to put a tactful question, changed his mind and said affably, "Megan, do you think perhaps a cocktail before we go . . . ? It's a miserable night. You'll join us, won't you, Mr. Sentry?"

So they were going to wait with him. Sentry nodded to the invitation and thought with savage pleasure, I can wait too. I can wait until Mr. Charles Farrar melts right back into the mold, and offered to help with the drinks.

Farrar refused assistance amiably. He said over his shoulder,

◈ 20

"I can't imagine what's keeping Sarah, unless—— Did she say she might go on to dinner, Megan?"

Sentry watched and listened politely, his face betraying nothing. Megan had the ball now, but apparently declined to run with it. "I really don't know, Charles, I only saw her for a few minutes this morning."

Silence, backgrounded by the splash of running water and the clatter of an ice tray in the kitchen; Megan Ware did nothing to break it. She seemed astonished by the number of well-manicured nails she had. Sentry glanced at her, realized with distant surprise that she was a good deal older and less demure than the childish hair would indicate, and went on listening tightly for the sound of a key in the door.

He remembered very clearly the last time he had been in this apartment. He had come on an errand concerned with Nick then, too. It had been Sunday, and snowing . . .

. . . Snowing. He welcomed the swirl of it, the bleak-fingered wind as he left the house on Barrow Street and went out into the early March dark. Behind him, in a bedroom upstairs, Tanner was talking casually and soothingly to his father, his alert physician's eye trained for any recurrence of the heart attack Christopher Sentry had suffered three hours earlier.

Sentry hadn't wanted to leave, had been afraid of the collapsed look on his father's staring face, but Tanner was firm. "Better go, Andrew, the sooner the better. He's got it on his mind and he won't rest until you do. Besides—the girl, whoever she is, has to be told sometime and it's only decent to do it at once. Go and get back; I'll be here and there's nothing to worry about."

Sentry couldn't find a cab, and after a few distracted efforts he began to walk in the direction of Washington Square. He noted with meticulous attention the weaving halos around the street lamps, icy chef's caps on the fire hydrants, white side streets channelling dimly away from him, nearly deserted in the Sunday silence. And recognized this half-consciously as a morbid desire to remember exactly the way things were on the day they learned that Nick was dead.

Nick was dead. The saying of it, the knowing of it needed time and practice, because he had been aware of his brother in a gradually deepening way ever since a foggily-recalled quarrel over a rocking-horse he was too small to mount. Thirty years, all told, and he had had only three short hours in which to try to realize that that was all. Conclusion. Not to be continued, next week or any other week.

What changes had there been in almost four years? How had Nick looked, how had he felt when—?

Sentry turned into Eleventh Street and passed the eternal symbol of New York, the man-walking-dog. Time was running out now, and in the next few minutes he must somehow manage to say in the gentlest way possible that Nick was dead, that Nick had been buried ten weeks ago in a prison camp in the Philippines.

He must tell this to Sarah Devany, who wore Nick's engagement ring; to Sarah, who had telephoned the house on Barrow Street yesterday to say in a voice that ran over with gayety and shook with the edge of something else that she had heard from Nick. The other postcard, over a year before, had gone to his father, and Sarah was half-crying at the sight of her name and address in Nick's handwriting.

"Andrew, I want to speak to your father in a minute, but he's all right, Nick's all right! I know they have to say that on these things, but it's his signature and it's dated—oh, damn . . ." Tears blurring an already blurred postmark; Sentry had gripped the phone, smiling. "Thank God. Take it easy, Sarah, here's Dad . . ."

That was the shocking, the horrifying thing, that there had been relief and exultation and excited plans for the homecoming of a man whose alien grave had long since been filled in and forgotten.

Here it was: the marble steps, the grillwork railings, the gilt-scrolled door; Sentry had almost passed the entrance in his sudden paralyzed loneliness. Was it four years, was it that long ago that Nick had said gravely, "Here we are. There'll be a plaque some day, but I'm trying to stall until I can get in on it, too"?

Sentry went down the steps and opened the street door and put his finger on the button opposite Sarah Devany's name.

The wait seemed eternal. As he stood with his fingers on the inner door knob, Sentry summed up an image of Sarah consciously, as though by doing so he could brace her as he was bracing himself against the impact of what he had to tell her.

He saw, almost as though she were there, the brief glowing mahogany-colored hair that ruffled along the white forehead; the serene gray eyes under dark brows with a delicate and permanent crook, the subtly-cut mouth that slipped easily from gravity to laughter. The things he couldn't see were just as clear. Impressions, because he hadn't allowed himself to gather much more; in the face of Nick's baffled and unuttered questions he had still felt firmly that, close as they were, a fiancée was one shared interest that could lead only to friction. Partly because he, who could at times slip inside Nick's heart and brain and nerves, must accustom himself to the fact that there was now someone with a prior claim.

But the impressions were there nevertheless—Sarah's shyness that could look like the chilliest hauteur, and the pride she battled with constantly. The impeccable quality of her love for

◆ 23

Nick, so that when they were together she made no excuses to touch him, and when the occasion arose managed it with such delicacy that no one except someone close to them both could know the electrical thing that had happened . . .

The buzzer sounded. Sentry let himself in and stood before the door of Sarah's apartment. The tentative phrases he had half-formulated went completely out of his mind, and he was wondering how he was to get the deadening words said to Sarah's expectant face when he noticed that the door was on the latch. Under the drive of a rising urgency to get his mission over with, he opened it and stepped inside.

He knew instantly that he had made a mistake.

A lifting and dropping mesh of voices, random laughter breaking through it, a constant stirring of figures in the wedge of living room visible from where he stood in the small foyer; Sentry realized with a feeling of nightmare that he had arrived in the middle of a party.

Go back to Barrow Street without seeing Sarah? Let her spend another evening, another night with the sunny conviction that Nick would soon be on his way home, that they would shortly be married? Every extra moment of innocence would be an added torture to her once she knew—and yet the prospect of telling her here, in the midst of a gathering that would immediately become a ghastly parody of the funeral baked meats, seemed equally impossible.

In the crowded room beyond him, a voice lifted above the others. "What in the world is keeping Gibby and Jane? They said they'd be here by six at the latest . . ."

Heads began to turn automatically in the direction of the door. Sentry, with every raw nerve wincing away from notice, took an involuntary step backward and found himself glancing through the partially open door of a bedroom.

◈ 24

At Sarah Devany, standing closely and obliviously in the arms of a man. Her shining head was cocked back so that her face tilted to meet his, and as Sentry watched the man gathered her tighter against him without lifting his head.

How long . . . ? Sentry knew later that only the flicker of a second could have passed before the betraying door creaked wider. At the time he was conscious only of staggering shock, and of his stomach turning hot and liquid with rage.

The tiny drawl of the hinge shattered the tableau in the bedroom. The man's arms dropped sharply away and Sarah thrust herself violently back and whirled and saw Sentry standing there. She said, "Andrew," put a hand to her cheek in a desperate gesture as though she might stop the sweep of hot color, and drew in a breath that seemed to take forever.

The blur beside her addressed himself to Sentry; he sounded half mocking and half defensive. "Oh dear. This is what happens, you see, to people who open doors without——"

Sarah stopped him without turning her head. "You'd better go, I think."

"Don't," said Sentry, forcing it past the revolt in his throat. "I really can't stay, Sarah. In fact, I just dropped by——" He made his voice, then, as brutal as he could, put into it all the cruelty of the War Department telegram, his father's terrifying seizure, his own lonely, agonized walk through the snow—"to tell you that Nick's dead. Shot—trying to escape. In December. Sorry to interrupt like this, but Dad thought you'd want to know."

He didn't leave immediately. He waited long enough to watch Sarah's eyes widen and stare and shut tightly in a face that drained slowly to the color of bone before her hands came up to protect it, to hear the whisper she wasn't able to shape into a word, any word. He thought detachedly that she was going to

◆ 25

fall. Then he turned and walked out of Sarah Devany's cocktail party.

". . . Here we are. Slow but sure," said Charles Farrar cheerfully, and put a glass into Sentry's hand.

He was not out in that snowy March night after all, sick and stricken under his anger; he was about to have a cocktail with two watchful strangers in a room into which Sarah Devany might walk at any moment. Any moment—the very imminence of it made his nerves draw still tighter.

Nick might just possibly have named his murderer. Messages had been known to come out of prison camp, coded in innocuous trivialities, invisible unless you looked for them. On the last postcard Nick had ever written—or on Sarah's memory of it—everything might depend.

Careful, Sentry warned himself, wanting to slam out of the apartment and comb the black rainy streets for the girl who was suddenly so important to him. He must be calm and reasonable when he faced Sarah, when he stepped onto the field with the enemy. With a deliberate effort he tore his listening attention away from the door, tasted the fruity, icy drink into which a small amount of rye had been allowed to creep, and glanced at the pair on the grape-colored couch.

Megan Ware and Farrar were chatting busily to each other with the over-expressiveness of two friends in the presence of an unknown third. They were on the weather now: "If you ask me, the farmers are at the bottom of it all." "Farmers, my dear Megan, are at the bottom of practically everything."

Sentry smiled dutifully and felt their eyes on him, sharp and speculative. Was Sarah, they were probably wondering, transferring her affections at this late date to her dead fiancé's brother? And if so, was it quite—becoming?

Sentry grinned without humor inside himself and thought, leaning against the mantel, that they were a cautious pair. Farrar, who had the soapy glow of a junior banker, looked like a man always soberly determined to do the right and decent thing—for the right people, under circumstances that would redound to his credit. And Sarah's cousin Megan, if appearances told anything at all, was more than anxious to do the right thing by Megan; her small face inside its frame of naïve and shining hair was knowledgeable and, when she forgot to be breathless, hard.

Was this, thought Sentry, watching them, a match perhaps? A wedding of self-interests?

On the couch, Megan stirred restlessly and turned to Farrar. "Do you think, Charles . . . ? I hate to disappoint you, Mr. Sentry, but when Sarah isn't back at this hour she's generally dining out. I'll tell her you were here, of course . . ."

"I'm afraid Megan's right," said Farrar, getting decisively to his feet. "You might waste a perfectly good evening for nothing. Not," he added affably, "that it's a very good evening. But still —Better get a wrap, Megan, we'll be late for the dinner show as it is."

A perfectly useless, worthless hell of an evening, thought Sentry, consumed momentarily with a flash of rage at Sarah Devany. He hesitated, halting the stir of departure around him in mid-flight, and was rewarded an instant later.

The lobby door closed distantly and there were voices in the hall. A man's, indistinguishable at first, emerged into ". . . better change your mind and have dinner with me. Women never eat anything when they're alone."

"What an interesting statistic, and how did you get hold of it?" said another voice, laughing. "No, honestly, James, thank you very much anyway. I'll call you about the Herberts' thing."

Sarah's voice.

Sentry felt as though he had been holding his breath. Charles Farrar and Megan, who had put a brief gold cape about her white shoulders, paused too, waiting for the crux of the odd little situation.

An exchange of goodnights in the hall outside; a key turned in the lock and the door opened. Sarah Devany closed it behind her and stood just inside the little foyer, darkly bright hair ruffled by the rain, gloved hands unknotting the belt of a very wet raincoat. She hadn't seen Sentry, her cousin and Charles Farrar stood between her and the length of the living room. She said, "I thought you two were off long ago. It's lucky you've got your car, Charles, the cabs have all gone underground, as usual," and stepped past them to put her gloves and bag on the desk and saw Sentry standing motionless on the hearth.

A second of time and six years of knowledge stretched between them like a rubber band. Sentry could feel the rise of a hostility to match his own in Sarah's still, endless glance down the room. But when she said, "Oh, hello, Andrew," there was no expression in her face at all.

◈◈◈ *4*

"WELL?" SAID SARAH crisply.

She had closed the door behind her cousin and Charles Farrar, and stood leaning one raincoated shoulder lightly against the square archway of the foyer. It occurred to Sentry, trying to clamp down his irritation, that she was trying for and achieving an air of brisk impermanence, of important things to be done after he had removed his delaying presence.

Good; it was better that way. State your business and go. Nevertheless, Sentry felt himself hardening. He had thought for an instant when she first came in that she looked white and a little bereft at the sight of the evening-dressed pair in her living room. That was nonsense, of course, because she had just turned down a dinner invitation of her own and he remembered now that she had always had that transparent pallor, the pallor that she had deliberately accentuated tonight by the slim black dress under the raincoat, the flat gold coins swinging from her small ears. In any case, Sarah Devany's emotional problems, if she had any, were no concern of his.

"I won't keep you," Sentry said without apology, his tone as short as hers. "It's about Nick, as a matter of fact. Have you still by any chance——"

Sarah interrupted him, only the tiny involuntary flicker of her dark brows showing that she had heard him at all. "Would you excuse me a minute? I'm rather wet."

The bedroom door closed behind her. Sentry lighted a cigarette and found that his palms were damp.

◈ 29

He had met Sarah several times since the evening six years ago when he had found her in another man's arms and had left her pale and swaying at his side. He had even thought, the first time, that there might be an explanation. There wasn't one. Against the bright smoky background of an after-theatre party, when the usual well-meaning fool had brought them together with hearty introductions, Sarah had said, "Mr. Sentry and I have met." She had given him a small cool nod, glanced indifferently over his shoulder and then moved past him to greet an acquaintance.

But then, and whenever their paths had crossed since, there had been people in the background—at parties, in an elevator, on the street. He hadn't met her on her own territory, where she provided the mood and the manner; hadn't labored before under the disadvantage of the self-invited. Most of all, he hadn't realized how much he would hate to ask anything at all of this girl.

The bedroom door opened and Sarah came in. She sat down in a small armchair near the hearth, lighted a cigarette and said composedly, glancing up at Sentry, "I'm sorry. You were saying——?"

"I wondered if you still had Nick's letters, or that last postcard." Even to his own ears the question sounded preposterous, and Sentry felt himself reddening. Before he could justify it Sarah said gently, as though she were explaining it to a forward child, "He wrote them to me, you know."

"I'm asking because there's a reason," said Sentry, controlling himself. "Have you?"

"Yes."

The letters. More vital, the postcard. And a chance, a good chance the more he thought about it—— "May I see them?" Sentry asked, and was unable to keep the grim exhilaration out of his voice.

◈ 30

Pause. It was not to be as simple as this. Sarah stirred in the lamplight, swung a narrow black-sandalled foot thoughtfully and looked up at Sentry. Reflected brilliance from one gold earring threw a tiny disk of warm color on her cheek. She said carefully, "I think, under the circumstances, that I have a right to know why."

Sentry hesitated an instant. In the brief time he had possessed it his knowledge had become somehow an enormously personal thing, absorbed into every cell, carried in his bloodstream. His instinct was to guard it as he would guard his own living vulnerable flesh, and to tell it would be to take a part of it away. But it had to be done.

In the moment while Sarah waited he had an intimation of himself as the familiar herald of disaster. He had come here the last time to bring the news of Nick's death; he was back now with an ugly postscript: the fact of Nick's murder. *Memento mori* . . .

He said in a voice that gave away information and nothing else, "I've been talking to a man who was in the camp when Nick was shot. It seems that it was—arranged deliberately, by someone who wanted him out of the way."

Sarah sat straighter. Her chin had gone up when Sentry began his answer, and shock stilled her head in its rigid backward poise. She said incredulously, "But you don't believe that!"

"Oh yes. My God, yes, I believe it," said Sentry.

And told her.

It became in his own mind clearer and a little more terrible in the telling. It was impossible not to see at least a part of the appalling life Nick had lived for three years, with the unheard-of becoming commonplace, the unbearable merely another degree of wretchedness. And then the finally-conceived

◈ *31*

plan for escape, thought around and lived with until it was almost certain of success. Until his personal doom came into camp.

Sands, who had murdered Nick. Sands, a killer in a place where bare existence was a day-to-day achievement, where sickness and starvation and brutality should have done his work for him. Sands, who with a few words to a guard had ended Nick's patiently fought-for life.

Sentry said quietly, finishing, "There are others who can back this up. Three men at least," and named them. "I'll see them, of course, but meanwhile there might be something in what Nick wrote, a mention of someone he'd known over here whom he ran into in the Philippines."

Sarah hadn't moved while he was talking; she had sat so still in the lamplight that it was difficult to know whether she was listening. Now she turned her head and gazed thoughtfully down the length of the room, her eyes shadowed. After a second of silence she said slowly, "Even if it were true, and even if you found—Sands, what could you possibly do about it?"

It was a question Sentry had looked at once in the darkness of his own mind and did not want to look at again. Not now. He took up the first part of the query instead. "In other words, you still don't believe it."

"I—don't know." Sarah put a hand to her forehead and brushed back the mahogany-colored hair. "You must admit, Andrew, that it's a bit wild on the face of it. You have a drink with a perfect stranger in a bar——"

Sentry held his temper back. "I didn't have a drink with him until he'd already mentioned knowing a Sentry. I was interested, naturally."

"And you don't think he might have noticed it and strung you along for a few more?"

"No, I do not think so. Next question?" It sounded childishly rude, but he was past caring about that.

"All right, next question." Sarah was calm. "I imagine things —impressions of people, trivialities—must get pretty distorted in a prison camp. Those men, the ones you say can back up this story, probably liked Nick. Most people," said Sarah, her voice scrupulously steady, "seemed to. Don't you think, after what happened, that they might have turned on Sands as a sort of whipping-boy for their feelings?"

Sentry took his shoulder away from the mantel, put his clenched hands in his pockets and said pleasantly, "No, I don't. That's what makes horse races, isn't it? As there doesn't seem to be too much point in all this discussion, may I have a look at the letters before I go? Unless you'd rather I took them with me and brought them back tomorrow."

Sarah stood up. She was trembling, and there was color in her face for the first time that evening, a faint furious pink. She said evenly, "Frankly, I would rather that nothing brought you back tomorrow or any other time until you've gotten over this ridiculous judge-and-jury manner of yours. It must be wonderful to be so sure of yourself when you put people away in their proper slots. Is it fun, Andrew? But then you have a really extraordinary gift, you can step into other people's skins and do the judging for them, too."

She stopped, staring at Sentry as though she were seeing an oddity for the first time. She said gently, "You know, Nick had manners and taste the way he had arms and legs and lungs. Isn't it—peculiar?" and swung away from him. "I'll get the letters."

Sentry watched her go, feeling as though he had been buffeted violently about the head, aware of a wry amusement prickling through his anger. He hadn't gotten an explanation of the scene in her bedroom six years ago but he had, he thought, heard her honest reaction to it. Resentment because it had been he who had glanced past that treacherously opening door, and a hint that Nick would have forgiven and forgotten.

But could Nick have forgotten the obliviousness of that embrace? Or the way, a moment later, Sarah had addressed the man at her side without looking at him, as though signals between them were unnecessary? Or the implied intimacy of her quiet order to him, which said plainly, 'Don't worry, I can handle this better alone'?

None of it mattered. Nothing mattered now but finding the man who had called himself Sands.

Sentry felt suddenly in his pocket and was relieved at the crackle of an envelope; on it, he remembered, were the addresses of the three men who might be able to help him in case Nick's letters could not. Twining, Pavick, Lyons . . . and they might lead him to others.

Where the devil was she? Sentry took a restless tour of the room, lighted a cigarette and threw the match into the immaculate fireplace. He was conscious for the first time of a dim surprise that Sarah had kept the letters at all; he would have expected her to erase cleanly and quickly all the things that had bound her to Nick.

. . . She was back. Walking down the room toward him, her burnished head high, her face as imperturbable as though she had never flashed at him in that lightning rage. With her hands, Sentry realized, empty.

She had changed her mind, then, during that interval in the bedroom; she had had time to build up her own resentment against him until Nick and Nick's murderer no longer mattered. Damn her, thought Sentry, and heard her saying, "I'm so sorry. I'd forgotten. They're up at my aunt's house, I'm afraid."

◆ *34* ·

It was a palpable lie. "That would be your maiden Aunt Martha, from the country?" Sentry inquired bitingly.

"I've told you I'm sorry," Sarah said, ignoring his tone. "I could send for them, if you like."

"Never mind, thanks." Sentry was already out in the little foyer, taking his raincoat and hat from the closet where Megan Ware had stowed them. Sarah didn't follow him; she stood like a poised black arrow against the chaste white and gray and blue-purple background.

Sentry nodded his farewell, said politely, "If you change your mind again let me know, will you?" and let himself quietly out.

It was still raining. Sentry headed back toward Fifth Avenue, his mind blank with disappointment. He hadn't realized until they failed to appear how much he had been counting on the letters, the postcard. But, short of conducting a forced search of the entire apartment, there had been nothing to do but accept Sarah's hasty tale.

She had obviously not been telling the truth. She wasn't a good liar; her eyes had challenged him while her voice apologized. She would have been perfectly capable, furthermore, of calling the police if he had attempted a search. She was within her rights, of course—standing just inside the margin and laughing at him.

It was nearly nine o'clock. Pavick and Lyons had had New York addresses; he would go back to his apartment and consult the telephone book. In case that failed there were the veterans' bureaus, the service clubs. Sentry boarded a Fifth Avenue bus, found a seat next to a large woman with a menacing hint of moustache, and remembered suddenly and hollowly that he had had no dinner. There were bread and cheese and coffee and cold beer in the apartment; better go straight there.

Somewhere between Eleventh Street and Thirty-eighth the rain stopped. Sentry stepped out into a night that curled coolly around him like giant leaves of silk, and began walking east. He was overwhelmingly tired all at once, flattened under the weight of the suspense that had been building up in him ever since the man in the bar had begun to talk. Tomorrow was Saturday—but no more late-sleeping week-ends now. Too much time, six years of it, had escaped already . . .

Sentry opened the door of his apartment and narrowed his eyes against unexpected lights. Cy Stevenson, big bumbling Cy in his untidy tweeds and round shell-rimmed glasses, put down a book and beamed at him from the depths of a slightly swamped-looking armchair. He said affably, "Come in, come in. Apartment belongs to a friend of mine, fellow by the name of Sentry, but I'm sure he won't mind."

Sentry grinned. "Hello, Cy." He threw his hat and coat into a chair. "How's the cheese supply?"

Cy made himself indignant, following Sentry into the kitchen. "What do you think I am, a rat? It's your cheese, you keep track of it. Look at the things the man has in his icebox—no wonder he comes home to eat. I take it you haven't eaten?"

The transition to awkwardly-covered solicitude was so familiar to Sentry that he smiled. "Nothing but a few crusts of bourbon. I could stand a sandwich, and some coffee."

He had met Cyrus Stevenson a few months after the news of Nick's death arrived, and had sought him out deliberately because he had learned that the other man had been at Camp O'Donnell before he was sent to Bilibid Prison. He had hoped then for more information about Nick, who had been at O'Donnell too, had even entertained for a time the fragile hope that the records at Cabanatuan had been mistaken. It was Cy who had found him his job as advertising manager at Ballard and

Sergeant, Cy who had watched him in those first few weeks when he drove himself grimly, staying at his desk until nine o'clock at night, not wanting to go back to the empty apartment and wakefulness and his crippling sense of loss. It was Cy who had made it his business to be aware of the time when Sentry snapped, and went blindly into a week of drunken nightmare.

Now Cy handed him a sandwich that bore the maker's trademark, bulging, generous, disreputable at first glance. He sat down opposite Sentry at the small kitchen table, his eyes shrewd behind the thick-lensed glasses. He said suddenly, "Listen, if you don't want to talk about it, don't. But take my advice, will you? Don't poke into it. Leave it strictly alone. You're not doing anybody any good and you'll just get yourself into a tailspin. Just because some guy you meet in a bar shoots his mouth off is no reason to——"

"Right," Sentry said brusquely. He got up and spooned powdered coffee into two cups and poured hot water. He knew he had sounded curt and ungrateful, but there could be no trespassing on these grounds.

This was between himself and Sands.

Hours later, with possible phone numbers written on a pad beside the telephone, Sentry lay awake in darkness and looked at a warped rectangle of reflected light on the ceiling. There hadn't been addresses to correspond with the ones the man in the bar had given him, but those had dated from six years ago. Tomorrow would tell.

Meanwhile, what was it that kept chasing elusively around in his head, something that came after "the snare of the hunters"? A psalm, almost certainly. His mouth drew down in the darkness: psalm-time with Sentry. Nevertheless, the same terrifying

imagery that had made him go solemn as a child persisted
now——

"Thou shalt not be afraid . . . of the arrow that flieth by
day; of the business that walketh in the dark . . . or of the
noonday devil."

Nick had eluded the snare of the hunters, had come safely out
of Bataan into prison camp. The day-by-day hazards of war had
left him alive and well enough to try for freedom; the shadowy
twistings and timings of chance—the bombed transport, the
group of prisoners who were promised hospitalization and then
taken around a curve in the road to be beheaded—had spared
him too.

But he couldn't, no one could have recognized the shape and
manner of death in a man who ate and slept and survived with
him against the common enemy.

Sands, thought Sentry, watching the rectangle of light flee
across his ceiling and out of existence; Sands, the noonday
devil.

Sarah Devany was trying hard not to look at the clock.

She washed her stockings, took a long bath, put on a thin
white silk robe and brushed her hair. Even so, the church bells
counted the time for her, the echoes naming themselves on the
damp windy night air although she didn't consciously listen.
Ten . . . eleven . . . twelve.

Twelve o'clock. It wouldn't be too long now. The bedroom
windows opened on the street; Sarah turned out the lights,
tilted the venetian blinds to let in the breathy coolness and sat
down to wait in the little armchair near the windows, tucking
folds of the robe about her bare feet.

Andrew Sentry's face swung up out of the darkness with the
expression it had worn when she had so unforgivably turned on

him; almost comical for an instant, with astonishment breaking through the mask of remote dislike. Andrew's face . . . Nick's face, really, with some amendments of his own: a small white scar disappearing into the dark hair over one temple, a line of impatience between the level eyebrows, a new bland way of smiling that had nothing to do with humor.

Andrew's face would always be disconcerting to her, because she had never thought she would learn to look for ice in Nick's dark slate-blue eyes, contempt in the mouth she knew so well.

Sarah got out of her chair, found and lighted a cigarette and went back to it in a rustle of silk. Why, why in heaven's name had she been such a fool as to fling away her only weapon, her pose of calm and complete indifference? She could not draw the arrow back out of the target now, she was as defenseless as she had sworn, six years ago, she would never be.

It had been the talk about Nick that had made her do it, of course; Nick and the way he had died. She had been honestly incredulous at first; now, coldly and horrifiedly, she knew that she was not nearly so sure.

Headlights went fingering along the opposite wall. A car had drawn up outside the apartment. Doors slammed, there was a low murmur of voices on the pavement. Sarah withdrew from the window, lingered restlessly in front of her bureau until she heard the sound of a key in the lock, and went back to the armchair, her hand on its way to the lamp switch. It stopped in mid-air.

Megan stood in front of the long mirror in its curly gold frame, her back to the darkened bedroom. As Sarah watched she pulled off one long white glove and lifted her bare hand slowly and caressingly to her cheek. The gesture drew a shining flash from the diamond on her finger.

So, Sarah thought dryly, mission accomplished. Charles

◈ *39*

Farrar, as per schedule, had put his neat head meekly into a noose of platinum.

She drew back sharply from her involuntarily watching pose and switched on the lamp beside the armchair. At the sudden dazzle in the mirror Megan whirled, dropping her hand quickly to her side, not dropping quite quickly enough her odd look of triumph. "Sarah! I thought you were asleep—did I wake you?"

Sarah shook her head. "I'd just put the light out. Have a nice time?" She would have to pretend not to notice the just-acquired ring, at least until she had asked a far more important question.

She waited in silence while Megan said casually, "Oh, very nice," went past her into the bedroom, put the gold cape on a hanger in the closet and crossed to the bureau to remove her earrings and bracelet. Then she said carefully, not meeting the enormous dark eyes in the mirror, "Oh, by the way, I've been looking for that stocking case I used to keep in the bottom drawer, the one with Nick Sentry's letters in it—you asked me about it once, remember?"

She paused and met the eyes in the mirror squarely, because at this moment she couldn't afford not to. She said, "It isn't there, it isn't anywhere. Did you take Nick's letters, Megan?"

◈ 5

MRS. PAVICK MADE no secret of her distrust.

She opened the door of the apartment wider to let Sentry enter, a thin depressed-looking woman with grayish-yellow circles under large alert pale green eyes. Sentry, walking past her into a small and rigidly neat living room, had an eerie impression that she might sting without warning.

"You might as well sit down," said Mrs. Pavick reluctantly, closing the door. She had already informed Sentry that her husband was out, in a tone that said his dark and significant errands were none of Sentry's business. He had seen this type of secretiveness before, in people who seemed to think that the most casual strangers were villains in disguise; that the magazine salesman, the census taker, the benevolent neighbor were all part of a base plot to steal the very roofs from over their heads. But they wouldn't, her manner implied, fool Henrietta Pavick.

A door across the room cracked open and a blond overalled child of about two peered solemnly out at Sentry.

"Jessie!" said Mrs. Pavick sharply.

"Wet," said the child simply, eyeing Sentry.

"Jessie!" It was tigerish this time, and the small face disappeared just as a fretful whimpering began in the room behind it. Against his will Sentry, who was now forcibly presented with himself as a kidnaper or at the least a molester of small children, found himself staring with an expression of fatuous fondness at the blankly closed door. Mrs. Pavick heaved a harassed sigh.

"Now she's woken him," she said, fixing the accusing pale green eyes on Sentry.

"How old are they?" inquired Sentry desperately.

He could see the calculation going swiftly over the long melancholy face. Free train fare . . . complaints about broken windows . . . was this a man from a photographic service? "Just babies, both of them," said Mrs. Pavick briefly.

The end of the road on that gambit. Sentry tried without success to efface himself on the small brilliantly-flowered couch and was relieved beyond measure when the door opened and John Pavick came in.

He had, it developed, gone around the corner for cigarettes, a dangerous admission which Mrs. Pavick could on no account have been expected to make. He was a big man, as blond as the child in the doorway, with a patient open friendly face. He said, "I hope you haven't been waiting long. Henrietta, did you ask Mr. Sentry if he'd like a cup of coffee?"

Sentry protested politely and in vain. He came straight to the point, uncomfortably aware that on Saturdays the Pavick household was given over to the endless duties connected with two small children.

"I'm sorry to break in on you like this. As I told you over the phone, I'm very anxious to get information about my brother. Anything at all that you can tell me . . ."

Pavick opened a fresh package of cigarettes, extended them to Sentry and took one himself. Not a deeply thoughtful man, but an honest and uneasy one, anxious not to inflict pain. He said, making a half-question out of it, "You knew that Nick was shot trying to get out."

"Yes." Sentry kept his voice dispassionate. "I've had one man's opinion that it was the work of an American, another prisoner."

He waited through a tense and endless moment while Pavick

relighted his cigarette, lumbered up for an ashtray, sat down again and said perplexedly, "Well, yes, we always thought so."

And there it was. Not that he had needed corroboration, not for the curious finality of his own belief. But this was not a fanciful man, nor one who would make passionate and empty accusations. Pavick's reasoning would have been slow and sincere, unswayed by any agitation around him.

Carefully, detachedly, Sentry took him through the story he had heard from the man in the bar; any emotion in his voice would, he knew, make the troubled Pavick shy away from details. He learned something he hadn't known before: that they had dropped Nick just outside the barbed wire, that he had spent the rest of the night in the guardhouse, wounded in both legs, that he had been shot the next day.

"To make an example for the rest of us. But they didn't shoot the Filipino well-digger," Pavick said, his face contracted with thought. "I guess they figured they needed him to dig wells. But with the beatings he got he couldn't have dug any wells for a long, long time."

Nick in a guardhouse, marking time until he died.

"They were like that, the Japs," said Pavick, considering it. "That's the way they treated the hens in camp, poor starved things that ate their own eggs just to keep alive. What d'you think they did? Reduced the rations for punishment. When that didn't work they beat the hens with sticks. When a thing doesn't obey you," said Pavick, unexpectedly savage, "you beat it, whether it's a train engine or a prisoner or a hen."

He couldn't add much more to the picture of Sands, except: "He snuggled up to the Japs right from the beginning, so that he got what soft jobs there were and they even had him helping out in the office a couple of times. He was put in charge of a work detail the day after they got Nick. And he cracked the whip more than most of the guards did—I know, because I was in his detail. Very diplomatic, Mr. Sands—or, I should say, Lieutenant Sands."

Sentry sharpened. "He was a lieutenant?"

"You could be a full colonel for all anybody knew," said Pavick. "Uniform was anything you managed to salvage. Your name—" he paused laconically "—was the name you gave the Japs who took you. I wish I could tell you more about Sands. He was dark-haired, I know that—even though he'd gotten hold of a clippers and shaved himself as close as you can do yourself. A lot of the men did that. I'd say off-hand he had a wiry build, but then," he grinned fleetingly, "so did I on a couple of teaspoonfuls of rice a day, and look at me now. He didn't have any of those strawberry marks you read about, either, that I never did see on anybody yet."

Sentry stood up. The question he didn't ask must have been there bitterly on his face, because Pavick said suddenly, "Hell, a Japanese pulled the trigger. What can you do? I thought about it, sure. But I spent the first six months after I got back trying to find a doctor who knew something about schistosomiasis, and a couple of months after that getting rid of it."

Hat in hand, Sentry asked Pavick if he could identify Sands after six years. Pavick had begun to shake his head dubiously when his wife appeared in the bedroom doorway, a fat and indignant baby in her arms. She was flushed with anger. "Now that's enough. My husband has tried to help you, Mr. Sentry, but we've got two children to think of. We can't get involved in anything like this."

In her mouth, Sentry thought, it took on the flavor of a poolroom brawl. He said constrainedly that he understood, thanked them both and let himself out into the hall. Pavick followed him, baffled and embarrassed. He kept his voice low, saying abruptly, "I'm sorry. The man you want is Bob Twining. He's the one who got the idea that Nick had something on Sands."

Sentry nodded. He said, "Dip Street, Chicago?"

"That's right. I got a Christmas card as usual. Bob's a good guy, even if I did think he was crazy that morning he told me about what he'd overheard."

Sentry halted at the top of five narrow flights of stairs. Pavick nodded soberly. "There was this business about not getting away with something, and what Nick would do about Sands when they got home. And then something about a trellis."

Sentry stared. "A trellis?"

Pavick nodded again. "That's what he said. I remember because it didn't make any sense then either. I guess maybe it never will. Well—sorry I couldn't help you more. Give my regards to Bob when you see him."

Had Twining dreamed the whole thing?

Sentry wrestled with that all the way back to his apartment; it shook him more than any of Sarah Devany's calm and logical objections. Even at first glance a convincing case could be made: a Japanese prison camp in December, a subject who was admittedly at a mental and physical low ebb, and half-sleeping but very real impressions of home and summer. Of a rose garden, perhaps, and trellises.

If only Pavick hadn't added that.

But wouldn't they have thought of a dream at once, Pavick and the man in the bar—oddly, he had forgotten to ask if Pavick could identify him—Twining himself? They would have realized even then that murder was a serious charge to bring against a man about whom they knew nothing, although, it was true, they had not brought it outside of their own small circle.

Sweating, Sentry reached his telephone and Long Distance. Twenty minutes later he listened to a bored operator's voice.

"I have an R.A. Twining at 2117 Dip Street. Would that be your party?"

"That's the one."

He heard the number given and wrote it down while a phone rang eight hundred miles away. But Saturday or not, former first lieutenant Robert Twining didn't appear to be at home. Sentry held on grimly, playing a childish game with himself: He's heard his phone ringing, now he's getting out his key, now he's inside the door—the operator put an end to this fantasy.

"They do not answer, sir. Shall I call you in an hour?"

Sentry hesitated, said he would try again himself, and hung up. A little over the allotted hour later he went through the same procedure, put back the receiver and sat staring at his living room wall.

It all hung on Twining now, Twining and—Sentry was unreasonably angry—his talk of trellises.

Go to Chicago and track down Twining there. Oh . . . Lyons, the third person in his little litany, had had a New York address six years ago. If he were to be accessible in an hour or so—— Character witness, Sentry thought wryly, and reached for the phone again.

Mrs. Lyons, when he located her at a Newark number after several calls involving queries shouted down elevator shafts and conferences held loudly in halls, sounded charming and a little amused.

"After all your trouble, Mr. Sentry, I'm sorry to say that my son isn't living at home right now. He's in Connecticut."

"Oh. Permanently?"

"As permanently as Gerald ever does anything. When last heard from he was working at a place called the Shoreline Club. I can give you the address if you like . . ."

◆ 46

The driveway of the Shoreline Club wove and curled its way for nearly a mile under a swinging sunlit ceiling of elm leaves. The golf course looked magnificent; the clubhouse itself, white-painted brick with clapboard wings, wore the faint shabbiness which is the badge of chic among established country clubs. A few guests were grouped idly on the wide shallow stone steps, a few more basked under the August sun on a flower-edged triangle of grass.

Sentry paid his taxi and went up the steps and into a broad cool hall whose shadowy spaces were punctuated by an occasional love seat and a few small flower-laden tables. At the far end of the hall a stairway curved up out of sight; to his left was what looked like a vast drawing room, occupied at the moment only by a graveyard hush. On his right, beyond a rib-high counter, was the office and a scene of complete pandemonium.

A large and terrified goat was cantering and clattering about among the desks, followed by a troop of whimpering stiff-legged kids who disentangled themselves into three. At Sentry's entrance the goat wheeled at the far end of the office and took a plunging leap at the barrier, hoofs rattling like stones on the composition. A man standing on top of the desk nearest the switchboard said politely, "Yes? Can I help you?"

The balked goat emitted a long nasal trembling noise.

"I'm not a member here." Sentry was confused to find himself saying it to the hairy agitated face glaring into his. He transferred his gaze, warily. "I'm looking for a man named Lyons, Gerald Lyons. I was told he worked here."

"Oh, he works here all right," said the man on the desk gloomily. He was tall and almost emaciated, with a narrow clever face and a faunish cluster of dark curls dipping into a high forehead. "In fact, you are now looking at Lyons. Lyons in the goats' den." He put a foot tentatively down on the seat of the swivel chair and snatched it back at a menacing caper of hoofs. He said beseechingly, "You know the old thing about sending a boy to do a man's work. What I want to know is, why am I always the boy they send?"

So this was Lyons. He was much younger than Pavick and the man in the bar, with a quick intelligence behind his mournful patter. Sentry wondered briefly if that lean stooping length could have survived the rigors of prison camp, or if this was the result. But someone, Cy Stevenson, had told him that it was the hearty super-athletic men who broke first, while the wiry ones pulled through.

In any case it was clearly impossible to talk to Lyons in his present setting. Sentry considered it while the switchboard buzzed and Lyons stooped double-jointedly, plugged in another wire and straightened again, looking harassed.

"This thing lifts up, doesn't it?" Sentry indicated the barrier, dubiously. "I could let them out."

"Lord *no.* The old party who owns this place would drop dead with rage. We're supposed to be having a Donnybrook Fair tonight and the goats are to lend a whimsical air to the office. They are now," said Lyons, surveying the rug with distaste, "er—rehearsing. Wait a minute, I'll try to get them out of here. What did you say your name was?"

Sentry introduced himself.

Lyons repeated his name blankly. "And there's something I can do for you? I don't think I——" He stopped abruptly, looked with full attention at Sentry and said slowly, "Hold on. You must be Nick Sentry's brother."

"Yes. That's why I came. There are a few questions I'd like to ask about the whole business."

"There would be," murmured Lyons, now frankly staring. "There would be . . . just a second." He lowered himself cautiously to a sitting position on the edge of the desk, plugged in a line, flipped a switch and said into the mouthpiece, "It's Lyons, Mrs. Biggs. Is Max around? . . ." And to Sentry, "Max owns the goats. He's the bell-boy. In fact he's at the bottom of this whole vile—— Oh my God."

A triumphantly flung hoof connected with an inkwell on the largest desk. Lyons looked hopelessly at a new river of black on the already mottled gray rug and said into the telephone, "Max? Listen, you've got to get up here right away and take these damned goats out of here. They've got me treed and they're tearing the office apart . . . The hell they won't bother me. Bring some ink-remover with you."

There was a stir in the hall outside. Three women in sunglasses paused on their way to the door, looked in and laughed, said, "Aren't they darling?" and went on their way. Lyons, still perched on the edge of the desk, hung up the receiver and said, "Max is on his way. I don't know about you, but I haven't had any lunch. Besides, it's quieter in the dining room."

It was. They had the big white-tabled room to themselves at something after two o'clock; the waiter grumbled as he took the order for Lyons' lunch and Sentry's beer. There were a few people lingering over coffee on the terrace just beyond french windows, and from somewhere came the hard repeated slap of a tennis ball.

Lyons lighted a cigarette and sat back, the clownishness gone from his long clever face. He said, "I probably have a hell of a nerve even asking this, but—is it wise?"

"For my purposes, yes."

"Your purposes," repeated Lyons. He cocked a half-mocking eyebrow at Sentry. "Vengeance is mine, saith the Lord."

"Vengeance?" Sentry made it surprised and a little deprecating. "That's not the point. I want to find Sands. I'm—curious."

Lyons' lunch arrived. He glanced down at it, murmured, "You'll never see a finer veal à la king," and gave Sentry a straight and piercing look out of sad brown eyes. "You've been primed. Who've you been talking to?"

"John Pavick. A man in a bar, about thirty-five, reddish complexion, almost a platinum blond."

"Blond. Not very tall? Might have been Church," Lyons said, his eyebrows going steep, "or that other guy, Hartman or Hartley or Hartwell . . . hell, I can't remember. One or the other of them had wife trouble, I think—two-wife trouble. Anyway, he put you on to Pavick and me?"

"And a man called Twining."

"Ah, Twining." The nostalgia was light and deliberately overdone; Sentry realized that the other man was trying to put the whole thing, for him, on a distant and impersonal stage. "Twining was probably lying awake, struggling with his conscience, when he heard what he heard—and I take it you've heard."

"Yes. I wondered if——"

"—he fabricated it, just for excitement? Or dreamed it? Not Twining," said Lyons, and now he was very sober. "In the first place, Twining had all the imagination of a Morris chair. True-blue, you know, but dull. He probably went through agonies before he could even bring himself to tell us about it."

Well, that was that. And Lyons was sensitive and almost abnormally observant. Sentry put a question and Lyons said thoughtfully, "I don't know. 'Trellis' . . . 'jealous'. The barracks walls weren't thick but they weren't transparent either. I know when I first heard it that's what I thought of—a woman in it somewhere. I warn you that that's totally unreliable, and probably only my prurient mind. But there you are."

A woman. Sentry wrenched himself away from a sudden inconsequential vision of Sarah Devany's shining mahogany-colored head cocked back for another man's kiss. He said evenly, "And—Sands?"

He had to control a tone of urgency, because Lyons was far and away the best witness he had had. The man in the bar had been blindly resentful, too late. Pavick was painstakingly sincere, too slow and too logical to pick up nuances. Lyons was one of those rare beings who are, often against their better judgment, receiving rods.

". . . Sands? It's hard to say." Lyons finished his lunch and looked up brightly at Sentry. "You get—warped. I spoon-fed a man next to me for weeks; he'd taken it into his head he couldn't survive anyway and he refused to take his rice, even when I sneaked him a succulent bit of rotten fish. He died eventually, and I was very indignant about my wasted effort. So you see . . .

"I'd say Sands came of what's generally called a good family. Money in the background, anyway, from his manner and a couple of things he dropped. And very fastidious, like a cat in a sewer. I got an impression he recognized Nick almost immediately, and that Nick didn't place him at all. Not for quite a while, anyway."

He paused while the waiter put coffee before him and removed Sentry's empty glass. "He—Sands—flared up over trifles. Much more than the rest of the men did, so it wasn't only camp nerves. He had a way of barking when he was angry or amused; believe me, it threw you off sometimes."

It was, Sentry thought, relaxing his attention for the first time, like the child's game in which you connected scattered points with pencil lines and emerged with a picture.

But this was not a game, and what was slowly taking form and direction was the shape of evil.

Sands. After less than twenty-four hours it seemed incredible

◈ 51

that the name hadn't always been there in his brain, the goad behind every impulse and action. Impressions were beginning to put flesh on the bare bones of it now. Sands was slowly assuming an identity.

A waiter came over to the table and delivered a muttered message to Lyons, who said, "Okay, Bert," pushed back his chair and glanced across at Sentry. "There's one other thing, but I don't know how useful it is. Before I got into the Army I worked as a stooge for a guy who had a small sustaining program, identifying people's accents from a few words they said into the mike—you know, Ozarks, Vermont, Maine, that kind of thing. I remember that whenever we got on the subject of backgrounds in prison camp, Sands talked vaguely about 'out West', but I'd swear he was a New Yorker, born and bred."

A New Yorker. Was it possible, then, that he himself had at some time been in a restaurant, ridden a subway, shared an elevator with Sands? And Sands, it was now certain, had recognized Nick instantly, because from the time he came into camp he had made himself faceless, meaningless, misty.

What would that face look like when he confronted it? Behind the borrowed name, whose face would it be?

Sentry thanked Gerald Lyons and tried to ignore a feeling of flatness. He had gotten what he came for, after all: the assurance that Twining, the fountainhead of everything, was not a man to imagine things. They entered the office through a door at the back; Lyons greeted a girl who sat at the switchboard and turned to Sentry, his faunish face half-questioning.

"You wouldn't be the first man to fish for a minnow and catch a whale."

"No. But I'm counting on a whale."

"Wait a minute," said Lyons abruptly. "If it's Sands' looks you're after, even a prison camp sketch might help. Pavick's in

New York, isn't he? Why don't you take Nick's notebook to him? He'd pick Sands out for you in a flash."

Sentry stared, conscious of a sudden hard pounding inside him. He said carefully, "I don't remember a notebook. They didn't send anything back, you know. We figured there was nothing to send."

"There wasn't anything else but that. It was one of the first things I did when I got back." Lyons was staring in turn; he looked incredulous and a little indignant. "I remember thinking his family might want it, so I took it over. He'd stolen it from a guard—you got so good you could even sneak rice out of their mess kits while they were eating—and he used it for sketching and i.o.u.'s, who he owed rice to in exchange for cigarettes, that kind of thing. I sent it registered first-class mail from Riverdale, which was where I lived then, and I can even tell you where I sent it because the address was on the last page and it stuck in my head. Mr. Christopher Sentry," said Lyons, concentrated and all at once grim, "Barrow Street, New York, New York."

6

SENTRY GOT A CAB at Grand Central.

He knew without caring that he ought to have called the
tenants at the Barrow Street house before descending on them
with a request to go through the old trunk in the attic. But too
much time had run out already, and even minutes could mean
people going out for cocktails, a phone ringing unanswered,
doors locked against the sense of urgency that made his head
ache. Minutes, which ticked into hours and eventually days,
could add up to ultimate defeat.

The Towers were at home and obviously expecting guests; in
a doorway beyond the gray silk figure of the maid who answered
his ring Mrs. Tower's expectant smile of greeting shaped itself
quickly into politeness instead. "Why, it's Mr. Sentry. Won't you
come in and say hello to my husband? Oh dear, I hope you
haven't come to tell us we can't put in a first-floor lavatory after
all. Did your agent get in touch with you——?"

Sentry explained his errand, said he would go straight up
without bothering anyone and mounted the stairs with the
peculiar sense of awkwardness and unease he had had in this
house ever since his father had died. As he passed the living
room he caught a glimpse of sunny cream and rose sprigged
chintz at windows where faded emerald velvet had hung.

The notebook wasn't in the old steamer trunk with the
crumbling straps, but he had been almost certain it wouldn't
be. He had packed his father's books himself, reluctant to dis-
pose of them at auction, seizing with relief on the lawyers'

opinion that a number of them would be valuable some day. In spite of his own conviction he searched methodically and unhurriedly, so that there could be no possible doubt. The notebook was small, after all; not quite as large as a child's composition book, Lyons had said, with a gray cover and ruled paper.

And on the ruled paper a sketch of a murderer, Sands.

Lyons had been positive about that. "Not that I ever saw one, but Nick must have done us all at one time or another—he'd do it in the barracks when the rest of us were flat on our backs, I guess it was his way of relaxing. But then he was an advertising art man, wasn't he? I saw a few of his figures, some of them were uncanny."

Was it possible that Christopher Sentry had thought the notebook would be a constant knife in them both, and destroyed it? Unlikely, thought Sentry, wiping dust from his hands.

If the notebook had arrived in this house and was not now among his father's possessions, it was much more probable that the old man had given it to someone. To Sarah Devany?

Sarah had come to the house once after the news of Nick's death; she had gone straight to Christopher, looking pale and desperately calm, and stayed with him for nearly an hour. That was when she had returned Nick's ring; Sentry, joining his father uneasily as soon as she left the house, had found him turning the magnificent diamond in its old-fashioned setting restlessly on his palm. "God knows I didn't want it, Andrew. But she said she knew it was your mother's and she felt it ought to stay in the family. Do something with it, will you? Put it away somewhere . . ."

Sentry refastened the straps of the trunk, swung himself down through the square opening that made the attic's entrance, and replaced the covering plank. New voices met him on the stairs;

the Towers' guests had come. Someone said heartily, "Now this is what I call a good drink," and Sentry, who had been about to slip quietly out of the house, paused in the downstairs hall.

Cy Stevenson turned quickly. His round face was momentarily blank with astonishment, the cocktail he had just tasted suspended in mid-air. Then he came forward, beaming. "Andrew, for God's sake! You in the second-storey business now? Whatever you took, put it back and we'll have a drink and say no more about it."

Sentry shook his head, smiling. "Can't, thanks, I've got to get back uptown. I didn't know you knew the Towers. Tell Mrs. Tower that I've gone, will you, and that I won't bother her again."

Cy nodded, his eyes only mildly interested behind the thick-lensed glasses. "Something about the estate, I suppose?"

"Yes. I don't know why old Penthrop couldn't come himself," said Sentry lightly, and was astonished at the smoothness with which the lie had produced itself as he let himself a moment later out of the house on Barrow Street.

He didn't need to call Sarah Devany.

His phone began to ring as he opened the door of his apartment. When he answered it he knew the clear steady voice as soon as it said his name.

"Andrew, it's Sarah. I've been thinking about what you told me last night."

"Oh. Yes . . . ?" Sentry made it carefully noncommittal, because if she had changed her mind about giving him Nick's letters too much eagerness might warn her away again.

He needn't have worried. Sarah was saying in the crisp neutral tone that put him instinctively on his guard, "You realize, of course, that if it's true, and if Nick actually did threaten this—Sands, then Sands must have been a criminal of some kind."

"It would seem to follow."

Again, as she had the night before, Sarah ignored the slight edge to that. She said coolly, "Then it's really a matter for the police, isn't it? Or the military authorities? Someone who could organize the kind of search there'd have to be, anyway. And have access to Sands' Army history, and all the rest of it."

Sentry looked at late sunlight lying ripely across the rug. He considered briefly and discarded explanations to Sarah: that official incredulity would be ten times her own, that even in the unlikely event of his being believed, any formal investigation would be interminable, intolerable months in the making. Most important of all, that this thing lay with a kind of hideous intimacy between himself and Sands.

He said instead, "There's no official evidence. There's nothing to put under a microscope. You could look me up ten years from now under Hysterical Relatives."

There was a pause at the other end of the line. The telephone in Sarah's apartment was, Sentry knew, on one end of a long low white bookcase; he had an uncanny vision of her sitting in the grape-colored slipper chair beside it, her arrogant eyebrows lifted a little, her face listening and imperturbable. Or did women bother to look imperturbable when they were alone? Or, for that matter, was she alone?

She said slowly, her voice blacking out his inner view of her, "You're going ahead with it on your own, then. It could be awfully dangerous, couldn't it?"

Who had said that so recently . . . Cy Stevenson, last night? Lyons, at the country club a few hours ago? Sentry answered her indifferently. "I don't know. By the way . . ." Cautiously, as naturally as he could manage it, he asked about Nick's missing notebook and described it. He could tell nothing at all from her immediate response. "No. No, I'm sure I'd remember if I'd ever seen it. I didn't, I know. Have you thought of looking up that man your father used to have . . . was his name Robert?"

It was. But unfortunately a good many other people answered to it, and Sentry had combed his memory all the way up from Barrow Street for the last name of his father's butler-valet-cook. The lawyers would probably be able to supply it. Sentry felt suddenly tired and as though he had thought his way temporarily into a closet; after Sarah had hung up he sat staring idly at the telephone and remembering the wartime company ads— Was this call necessary? Sarah had had nothing to say, and she had said it with her usual air of dislike behind formal politeness. Why had she bothered at all?

Unless she had the notebook and was curious as to whether he had found out that there was one.

Well, now she knew, if that had been her object. She had sounded oddly truthful in her denial of having seen it, but then she had obviously lied about the letters and the telephone might have been invented for liars. Sentry lighted a cigarette and abandoned his search into Sarah Devany's motives; she was too accomplished an adversary for that.

His feeling of weariness persisted, although it wasn't quite seven o'clock. But it had been a churned-up day; he had seen Pavick and Lyons and, peculiarly, Cy Stevenson. Cy had never spoken of the Towers—but that was one of those things, thought Sentry; people sometimes felt that friendship went awkwardly with business. Cy had known the Barrow Street house was on the market and had produced the Towers as tenants without mentioning an acquaintanceship, for that simple and often sensible reason.

There was food in the kitchen but the apartment was suddenly full of imponderables. Sentry located his hat and went out in search of dinner.

It was nearly nine when he returned. The second airlines he called gave him a seat on the ten o'clock plane to Chicago the next morning. Sentry wrote down the flight number and left the telephone, resisting an impulse to try Twining again. The man in the bar had disappeared abruptly once he knew the direction of Sentry's questions; even the perplexed and sincere Pavick had been driven to silence by his wife's intervention.

Sentry opened every window in the apartment against the sultry night, made himself a drink, smoked two cigarettes and went to bed. By the time the flapping curtain put him to sleep he had evolved several violent and impractical schemes for burgling Sarah Devany's apartment.

As he had the night before, Sands came like a mist to take possession of his dreaming brain.

They landed in the rain, late. Sentry walked up the ramp with the worst case of nerves he could remember since Cassino. He had felt, watching the dawn sift in, like de la Mare's "one man left awake"; he had gone over the coming interview a thousand times in his mind, knowing he was expecting too much of it.

In the main building at the airport he found the last unoccupied phone booth and dialled the number he had written down the morning before. He said to the male voice that answered, "Mr. Twining?"

"Yes."

Sentry couldn't have formulated the random fear that had overtaken him in the plane; he knew now, by his terrific sense of relief, that it had been this.

He said, "My name is Sentry. You don't know me, but I came as soon as I heard——"

"Of course," said the other voice, interrupting.

Sentry drew back from the down-tilted mouthpiece—why did public phones always look as though they had last been used by a pygmy?—and stared at it in astonishment. After a second of blankness he said, "I'm at the airport. I'll get a cab now," and hung up.

Inside the taxi, with rain weaving down the windows, he wondered who had seen fit to warn Twining of his arrival. Had it been Pavick, or Lyons—or his original informer, the man in the bar? The odd part of it was that Twining had seemed neither warm nor cold, eager nor hostile; he had sounded merely tired and a little snappish. Time, less and less of it now, would unravel that. Sentry lighted a cigarette with the vague notion of dissolving the cornerstone in his stomach and began to look out the windows. He realized when the cab drew to a halt that he hadn't seen anything at all.

Dip Street was compounded of trolley tracks, gas stations and apartment buildings with delicatessens cornered in them. Faded gold letters on the door of a yellow brick façade announced Twining's address. Sentry went up steps and into an outer lobby, found Twining's name opposite 5C, and was admitted with a loud clicking sound to the Stygian darkness of the inner hall.

The self-service elevator was old and dim. Sentry pressed the fifth-floor button and began a clanking and interminable rise. Halfway up he took out a cigarette and put it back again; he would save that gesture for sometime in the next two minutes.

It was less than that. As the elevator doors crashed shut behind him another door opened at the end of a shadowy hall. A man's figure was blocked against watery light from a window over the stairs. His voice was the one Sentry had heard earlier on the telephone. "Is that . . . ? Oh. Mr. Sentry?"

Sentry's first reaction was shock and embarrassed pity; even in dimness he could see that Twining's face was ravaged and his hair nearly white. He reached the end of the hall and the man stepped back to indicate the open door of the apartment, and dull wet light from the window struck directly across his face. He was a man of at least sixty.

Twining's father, Sentry told himself, walking mechanically past him; it's all right. But he knew from the older man's stiff dark suit, the strain around the tired eyes, an incongruous scent of flowers, that it wasn't. He waited silently.

The other man closed the door and turned to Sentry with weary politeness. "Nice of you to come, Mr. Sentry. I'm Bob's uncle—George Twining."

It said nothing and everything, and he still had to ask. Sentry said, having to force the unnatural shortening of the name, "Bob's dead?"

George Twining's face woke briefly to surprise; it was as though the tiny final phrase were still too new to be acceptable. He said confusedly, staring at Sentry, "I'm sorry. Yes, I thought you knew. You said when you called . . . I wondered how you'd heard so soon when he—when it was only last night."

Sentry looked away from the fresh bewildered grief. He said gently, "I'm very sorry. I had no idea at all. I came from New York in hopes of seeing him, as a matter of fact." He stopped, wondering if there were any decent way to ask questions. He had gotten as far as a cautious "Would you mind——" when the other man cocked his head at a distant sound and stood up abruptly. "That'll be my niece—Bob's sister. You'll excuse me a minute?"

Left alone, Sentry stared at looped-back curtains, a violin in an open case in one corner—had Twining played it?—massed flowers and fern with a smiling pastel look of death. He remembered his own bleak early-morning hours, the sudden shapeless dread that had seized him in the plane, the relief he had felt in the phone booth at the airport. Robert Twining had been dead all the time . . . how?

The returning footsteps reached the door. Sentry rose, not wanting to ask the questions that would seem to these people brutal, knowing he must. The door was pushed wide and George Twining came in with a tall sandy-haired woman whose squarish and rather plain face might have been domineering forty-eight hours ago. It wasn't now. She gave Sentry a docile nod when introductions were made—her name was Margaret Twining—and turned back to her uncle.

"They want you down at Jessups' with—clothes. I thought the gray suit—his new one," she said steadily, "and whatever tie you think."

Sentry had begun to perspire. He was wondering if he could really stick this out when Margaret Twining watched her uncle disappear into a bedroom, came back to the couch, sat down and said with determined briskness, "I understand you wanted to see my brother, Mr. Sentry. As you've come all the way from New York, is there anything I can do to help you?"

"No—but I was about to ask you that," Sentry said awkwardly. At the small shake of her head he made himself say, "Would you mind very much telling me what he died of?"

It seemed an endless instant, an unbearable stretch of waiting before she answered him. "He was struck by a hit-and-run driver, they think about two o'clock this morning. He was—he'd been drinking heavily. I knew that myself when he called me up last night—I was visiting a cousin just outside the city—to tell me he'd met up with an old friend and they were going out to celebrate."

Sentry watched her. Her face had sharpened with new aware-

ness of loss; for a moment or two she had been almost unconscious of a listener. Her eyes were too wide and a little glazed.
It was the looking-back time, Sentry thought, the terrible tele-
scoping of all the blundering words, all the punishing silences.

When her voice stopped, he repeated carefully, "An old
friend? Someone you knew too?"

"Oh no," said Margaret Twining.

The bedroom door opened and her uncle emerged with a
small suitcase. Even though he went quickly and quietly to the
door and let himself out at once, the burial garments were
shockingly present. They gave Sentry the courage to go on after
a stricken silence had fallen over the small room.

"Your brother didn't say, then, who——?"

"But he did," she said clearly. "He—you know how men are."
There was a dreadful instant in which they both knew that she
would never know how that particular man was again. She went
on with a painful brightness, "He was just like a boy about it,
really—I suppose it makes more of a bond than most things.
He'd just found a man he was in prison camp with, whom he
hadn't seen in years. I think he said the name was Sands."

7

AFTERWARDS, SENTRY FOUND his own true north like a magnetic needle; the bar was small and the bourbon fraudulent, but he had never wanted a drink more urgently.

'Like a boy about it, really . . . makes more of a bond than most things.' The liquor went sour in his mouth when he thought about that. A real old Army reunion. Death hadn't only caught up with Twining; he had gone out buoyantly to meet it. Had forgotten, perhaps, the clarity of the betrayal at Cabanatuan, or dimmed it deliberately, caught up in the inevitable urge for old companionships.

Margaret Twining had shown him a photograph of her brother, and Sentry had thought, looking at it, that Lyons' description seemed to fit. Sturdy, solemn, unimaginative—it could be read easily into the straight sober gaze, the earnest mouth, the faintly accusing eyebrows.

That was the trouble, he thought now; Twining had never realized his own appalling danger, even though he must have known more than he had told about the conversation outside the barracks in the Philippines. Enough, at any rate, to be a threat to Sands, once questions were raised about the manner of Nicholas Sentry's death.

How had Sands known that questions were being raised?

Sentry finished his drink and left the bar. Two blocks north he found a florist's shop, racked his brain for the name of the funeral home and recognized it in the directory obligingly supplied. He thought, as he went out again, that twenty dollars' worth of flowers was a poor apology for sending a man to his death.

The rain had stopped but there had been cancellations for the next flight to New York. At the airport Sentry got a seat on the five o'clock plane and sat down on a bench to wait, conscious of a thin exhilaration.

Sands had wiped away Twining's evidence forever, but in doing so he had shown a light of his own. Only a very small and definite group of people had known that Sentry had discovered the six-year-old murder of his brother and was on his way to talk to the man who could tell him more about it.

Sentry began to count the names, the voice in his mind drowning the crisp echo of the loudspeaker, blotting out the flow of people around him.

He skipped over Pavick and Lyons because each of them had been clear in the other's account. He was increasingly sure about the man in the bar. Wife trouble, two-wife trouble, Lyons had said—it wasn't unheard-of in wartime. It would explain more simply than anything else his confidant's sudden plunge into anonymity.

Go on from there, then. He had mentioned Twining to Cy Stevenson and to Sarah Devany, whose cousin Megan Ware had undoubtedly asked questions later. If the match between Miss Ware and Charles Farrar were as imminent as it looked, there was Farrar, almost certainly. Throw out Cy——

No, thought Sentry coldly. Throw out nobody.

One of those people was in touch with Sands.

Or was Sands.

"Kettle," said Mr. Penthrop briskly. "Robert Kettle. Is it something we can handle for you, Andrew?"

"Thanks, but I want to look him up anyway."

"I see. If you'll hold on just a minute I'll have his address for you . . ."

Sentry held on. It was Monday morning, and beyond his windows the air was buttery with heat. Check the notebook first, if possible; he would know better then what stand to take with Sarah.

Waiting for the address of his father's valet, he lighted a cigarette one-handedly and stared at the floor. It seemed odd, in spite of all his calculations, to realize that Sands was somewhere very near him, that Sands ate and slept and bathed just as he did; might, in fact, be breakfasting at this moment. With Twining's death Sands had stopped being a shape of evil, a weight of knowledge that made Sentry wake rigid in the night. He had become a physical man, a murdering entity close enough to Sentry to know his movements . . .

". . . Sorry to keep you waiting," said Mr. Penthrop at the other end of the line, and recited a Harlem address. Evidently feeling that a sentiment, however vague, was called for, he added, "A good man, Robert. He served your father well."

But can he, thought Sentry, agreeing and a moment later hanging up, be expected to remember the arrival of a parcel six years ago?

Surprisingly, Robert did.

Sentry found him at home in a small spotless bachelor apartment, just finishing his breakfast. Without his white coat and his air of being able to produce magical comfort at a moment's notice, Robert looked old and doubtful and worried. But when Sentry, searching for conversation on his arrival, commented on the pleasantness of the apartment, Robert said calmly and without the hint of a wink, "Thank you, sir. I have a person who —obliges."

He remembered the arrival of the parcel very well because of Christopher Sentry's reaction to it. It had come, Robert thought, about three weeks after the news of Nick's death.

"It was two days before your father had his first stroke and went to the hospital, and to this day I can see the sad look he gave me when he saw it. And he said to me, 'I'm afraid we'll have to brace him for this, Robert'—meaning you, sir."

Had that been the one small extra burden his father couldn't take alone? Sentry said, "Did you get a look at it, Robert?" and sensed a tiny immediate withdrawal in the severe dark eyes on his.

"No, Mr. Sentry, I did not. I did see that it was all tattery, but in a minute or two Mr. Sentry put it away in his desk, and that," said Robert with dignity, "is the last I saw of it until you sent the messenger for it and I gave it to him."

Sentry went home with his cold controlled fury several notches nearer the surface.

Impossible to blame Robert, who had acted in good faith on what he had thought were Sentry's instructions. Sentry himself had taken a hotel room in order to be near his father's hospital, and in the last days of waiting and anxiety before his father died, and later during the confused period of readying the Barrow Street house for rental, the incident had slipped from the valet's mind.

Sands' maneuvers were clear instantly. In the confinement of the barracks at Cabanatuan, Sands would have known about the notebook Nick used for sketching, but would not have dared to steal and destroy it then and there. When Lyons had announced his intention of sending it to Nick's family, Sands had made his plans accordingly, and luck had been with him all the way.

◈ 67

Perhaps a day or two of watching the Barrow Street house, and presently a phone inquiry, forgotten among countless others, which told him that Christopher Sentry was critically ill, that his son was not at home. Then another call, brisk, commanding, intentionally muffled: "I'm sending a messenger for that notebook of Nick's that came the other day—my father wants it right away."

Impossible to blame Robert, equally impossible to forget that Sarah Devany had visited Christopher Sentry the day before he went to the hospital. The day after the notebook arrived. Had Sands been sure in advance that Lyons and the notebook had already reached the United States? Or had he learned it from Sarah Devany?

A shower and the last cold beer in his icebox were reviving. Sentry was weighing the desirability of going out into the heat for more cold beer to revive with all over again when Cy Stevenson called to ask him to lunch. Cy sounded urgent. He had probably begun to be embarrassed about the meeting in Barrow Street, Sentry thought, agreed to a restaurant off Fifty-first Street and said he would be there at one o'clock.

Cy was late. Sentry sat down on a leather banquette behind a table apparently designed for people who drank out of thimbles, and ordered beer. He was turning the glass idly in his hand and wondering whether they would bury Robert Twining that day when an injured voice directly in front of him said simply, "Hey."

Sentry glanced up, startled, and forced a grin. "Sorry, Cy. I didn't see you in all this high-priced gloom."

"All you can do to find your hand before your face," agreed Cy, but his eyes were shrewd and worried. He nodded at Sentry's glass. "Can you bring that with you? . . ."

They were halfway through lunch before he mentioned the

Towers. "Eloise—Mrs. Tower—gave me hell for not making you stay for a cocktail. She didn't know I knew you, and I had to back out of that one fast. The fact is that I thought the less camaraderie all around, the better—you might want to turn them out in the snow some time and then where would you be?"

Sentry said casually that they seemed like nice people and Cy said they were. A few minutes later he started circuitously toward what was evidently the point of the luncheon. "Did you see that fellow, what was his name, in Chicago?"

"Twining. No," said Sentry without expression. "He's dead, as it turns out." He watched the man across the table, telling himself that it was absurd, remembering that someone who had known about Twining had flown to Chicago to kill him. He saw only mild sober surprise on the round face.

"Really? Must have been a shock, when you'd been counting on him—he was more or less the end of the trail in this thing of yours, wasn't he?"

"More or less."

"Well," said Cy after a second's silence, "I'd be making a liar out of myself if I said I was sorry. It's a damn good thing you've run out of leads, if you ask me. Take it this way—if this business about Nick isn't true, you're pulling yourself through knotholes over nothing. If somebody did engineer it, it might get to be a habit of his with the Sentry boys."

When Sentry said nothing he went on, "Listen, what you need is a vacation. Swimming, sunburn, poison ivy—the works. I've got a little place up in Swannet that some cousins were in up until a week ago. There's nobody there now. Why don't you take off and get yourself a rest?"

Sentry shook his head. "Thanks, but not now." He smiled. "Don't worry about me, Cy, you won't have to play nursie this time. I know what I'm doing."

Cy looked distressed. He said finally, "Well, if you're hell-bent on staying around, what's to prevent your taking a job? Hewitt rugs, you know them, they used to be a stepchild of Hewitt Industries, have had a shot in the arm. They're cooking up a national campaign, Epperson there told me about it. They're looking for a man."

Sentry shook his head again. "So am I," he said.

SENTRY HAD gotten to hate the sight of his apartment.

He had liked it very much at first; it was easily accessible and still far enough removed from the tumult four blocks west of it to be relatively peaceful. But the solitariness, the being alone in his own domain that had seemed so pleasant then had now become a weapon. The silences kept filling up with questions, with a maddened sense of time slipping by while he did nothing, with the things he had learned about Nick in the last three days.

Nick in the guardhouse, waiting out the night, knowing that the morning's object lesson was to be his own death under ceremonial rifle fire. Not buried in the camp by Americans, like other prisoners who had died from illness or starvation, but taken by the guards to a grave in the cogan fields beyond the barbed wire.

Nick must have known his betrayer then, must have had that to bear, too: the knowledge that Sands would watch the execution with the others and then return quietly to the barracks, suitably sober, suitably regretful.

But—this was the pivot of the whole thing—had Nick recognized Sands by the time he had sent the postcard to Sarah?

Talk to Sarah. Put her off her guard, frame some sort of apology for the way he had broken the news of Nick's death at her cocktail party six years ago. Find out whom she had mentioned Twining and his own suspicions to—and, if she were sufficiently disarmed, get the letters and the postcard.

It couldn't be done all at once; he knew the measure of her hostility by his own. He would have to win her confidence by degrees, pretend a mutual misunderstanding in the past and an acknowledgment now of the bond between them. Take her out to dinner, perhaps . . .

He found that the thought of paying small attentions to Sarah Devany was as alien as though he had been asked to perform tribal rites at a Borneo wedding. Only a growing conviction that she could lead him to Sands took him to the telephone at a little after six o'clock.

It was Megan Ware who answered, her light, slightly breathless voice sounding a little disappointed. "Oh, Mr. Sentry. Just a minute, I'll call Sarah."

There was a long flat silence in which Sentry, waiting, could imagine Megan being primed and sent back with an excuse. Sarah's crisp impersonal "Hello?" made him start.

"Andrew, Sarah."

"Oh. You're back from Chicago, then."

No, thought Sentry annoyedly; no, I'm still in Chicago and unfortunately I haven't been able to get to a phone. He said, sounding falsely hearty to himself, "Yes. Would you by any chance be free this evening, Sarah? If you are I'd like to drop around and talk to you for a few minutes."

Pause; she was apparently examining this for the hook in it. But she was curious; she said at last, "Yes. That is—yes."

"Fine," said Sentry. "When?"

"Oh . . . about eight?"

"See you then," said Sentry, echoed her still faintly surprised goodbye and hung up.

The church bells were striking the hour as he turned the corner into Eleventh Street. Sentry stopped and lighted a cigarette and slowed deliberately, feeling more than ever like a high-school boy on his first date. It would be pleasant, he thought grimly, when this was over and Sarah Devany could be dropped cleanly out of his life again. Meanwhile there was nothing to be gained by antagonizing her, and everything to be lost.

He passed the dentist's sign, the window-box with the flowers in it blanched by darkness. He entered the door of Sarah's building with all his old reluctance, pressed the buzzer, went in into the hall and found Sarah standing in her doorway.

She was wearing something the cool color of lilacs. There was a faint trace of pink in her cheeks. She looked, thought Sentry, half-amused at his recollection of two nights ago, as though she had been quarrelling with someone. She wasn't alone, there were voices from inside the apartment.

They belonged, he found an instant later, to Megan Ware and Charles Farrar. There were cocktails in progress. Sentry noted idly that Megan's glass was empty, Farrar's nearly full. That could mean that Farrar had just arrived; that Megan's disappointment over the phone had been because the call was not for her, that Sarah had had an opportunity to quarrel very recently with her cousin.

Or that Megan was a quick drinker.

But there was tension in the room, obvious even to someone who was a comparative stranger to all of them. Sarah asked Sentry politely if he would like an old-fashioned and then, when Farrar was on his feet, went quickly into the kitchen herself. As though she were glad to go, thought Sentry, puzzled.

Megan Ware leaned forward a little on the couch, and he noticed for the first time that she was dressed as though for a journey; pale lemon suit nearly the color of her hair, an enormous leghorn hat, white gloves and bag on the table beside her. She said demurely, "I understand you're just back from Chicago, Mr. Sentry. Pleasant trip?"

A tiny shock of anger went over Sentry. He had realized that Sarah would have made some explanation of his presence in her apartment the other night; he hadn't expected that it would be turned into social chat. Particularly if one of these people had talked.

Megan was still watching him; the unwavering intentness on the small pointed face was oddly disconcerting, as though an old and cynical cat were looking out of kitten eyes. Charles Farrar had turned his neat dark head inquiringly. Sentry said pleasantly, "Not so hot, Miss Ware. What you might call a frost, in fact. The man I went to see was dead when I got there."

In the kitchen the small click of ice against glass stopped abruptly. Megan Ware's gaze stayed wide and fixed. The only stir in the room was the fractional movement of Farrar's head as he turned to look at her.

The clatter of an ice tray in the kitchen shattered the moment. Megan's brows went up as she said, "Oh, that's too bad," in conventional distress, and Charles Farrar removed his stare to the rug and shook his head a little, sympathetically. Sarah came into the room with Sentry's drink, and he could almost have been convinced that he had imagined the reaction, sharp, definite, in at least one of his listeners.

It was only a few minutes later that Megan said, "We'd better be going, Charles, don't you think? Dinner—and you know how I am about trains . . ."

They both stood. Charles Farrar circled the couch and lifted three pieces of matched navy and white luggage Sentry hadn't noticed before. He did notice, because it was clearly there, the stiffness with which Megan said, "Thanks so much for everything, Sarah. You've been terribly kind. I hope I'll see you——"

◈ 74

"Oh, you will," Sarah said. She was standing, too, taller than Megan, very cool and poised in the wide-skirted lilac dress. "Aunt Harriet asked me up for my vacation, you know. I'm starting it Wednesday, so I'll see you both in Swannet quite soon."

It was said casually; why did it sound like an ultimatum? Sentry, who had started a little at the mention of Swannet, where Cy Stevenson's cottage was, heard Megan say flatly, "How nice. Well, we're off. Goodbye, Mr. Sentry, thank you again, Sarah . . ."

As they moved toward the door Sentry caught a last glimpse of Megan's small face, hard and—was it resentful?—in its frame of straight soft hair. He thought briefly that if he lighted a match the room might very possibly explode, and stopped wondering abruptly as Sarah closed the door after her departing guests and came back into the living room.

She glanced abstractedly around her for a moment, met Sentry's eyes, said, "I think I'll make myself a drink after all," and went out into the kitchen.

Sentry followed her. Kitchens were supposed to be easy and companionable; this one, at the moment, was plainly not. Sarah seemed unaware of his presence. She spooned cracked ice and a minimum of sugar, measured bourbon, added bitters and a twist of lemon peel and picked up her drink, stirring it absently. She said, her head still bent, "I heard what you told the others about the man in Chicago. It's too bad, isn't it?"

Sentry drew a long gentle breath. He said containedly, "Yes, I thought so. He must have been rather taken aback by it himself. If there was time."

Her head came up sharply. "Time . . . ? What do you mean?"

Sentry told her, wondering what was going on behind the steady gray gaze. He said, finishing, "His family are satisfied that it was an accident. So are the police, apparently. A hit-and-run driver, a pedestrian full of neutral spirits—the circumstances aren't exactly rare. In fact, if it weren't for the telephone call to his sister, mentioning the Army friend . . ."

Sarah shook her head a little, wordlessly, and the ruffle of hair along her forehead caught a glow from the ceiling light. She said levelly, "Oughtn't the police to know about the call, then?"

"There's nothing to open a case with. He'd admittedly been drinking. And the non-appearance of his ex-Army friend would look quite plausible—people seldom like to be involved in fatalities even when they're accidental. I can imagine how far I'd get—particularly when his family are all settled about how it happened."

They were back in the living room, Sentry leaning against the mantel, Sarah in the slipper chair she had occupied three nights before. She was clearly shocked out of her hostile composure. Sentry looked detachedly down at her; she was staring at fingers she had locked like a frightened child, her drink ignored on the table beside her. Well, thought Sentry a little dubiously, here we go.

He lighted cigarettes for them both. He said with a tentative air, "You know, we can't completely rule out the possibility that Sands is someone one of us knows. For instance, he's had to have found out I was going to see Twining and ask questions about what happened at Cabanatuan."

"Someone we——"

Sentry rode gently through the attempt at refusal. "Twining was allowed to live for six years, remember. Maybe he'd agreed not to talk. Maybe he just wasn't much of a talker. But direct questions would be something else again, or so Sands thought.

The point is that he couldn't have plucked this new threat out of the air."

Sarah had tasted her drink and seemed to find it steadying. She said almost argumentatively, "Then whoever—he'd have had to fly."

"It takes under four hours."

"The airlines might——"

"I had a try at that. Sands would hardly have been stupid enough to use either his real or his prison-camp name, though, and they don't produce passenger lists just for the asking. I suppose your cousin would have known about Twining, for instance?"

The startled glance she gave him turned mocking for an instant. "She was rather curious when you turned up so—abruptly the other night. I think I told her you wanted the address of a friend of Nick's in Chicago and thought I might have it. But I can assure you that Megan does not shave daily."

Be nice to this girl.

"I didn't think so," Sentry said, smiling over clenched teeth. "Can we presume that Miss Ware confided in Mr. Farrar?"

"She may have. They're engaged again. But Charles wasn't even in the Philippines. Wherever he was," Sarah said, suddenly defensive, "he had a bad time of it. He was invalided home before the end of the war and spent three months afterwards in a sanatorium."

And that, Sentry said to himself, would explain Farrar's oversupply of self-importance, his tendency to take control of the most casual situations: he was trying too hard to live up to and beyond what the doctors had advised. Underneath somewhere there was still a layer of uncertainty, a hidden region where he had cracked up.

"Tough," he said mechanically, noting that Sarah obviously did not know where Farrar had spent the war years. "Anyone else you can think of, Sarah? Just to clean up all the possibilities?"

"Only one other person." That much off-handedness, that lucid a gaze must indicate defiance. "I told a friend of my family's—he'd met Nick years ago, too. His name is James Court. After what you said the other night, I was naturally anxious to find out what I could, and as James saw Nick once for two days at Cabanatuan——"

Sentry didn't hear what she had thought; he was meeting astonishment in a new quarter. For an instant the prison camp seemed like a secret society he hadn't been voted into. He stopped struggling with a fresh rush of conjecture in time to hear Sarah saying coolly, "—and besides, James was with me Saturday evening."

Sentry didn't analyze that; the words slid off his consciousness and left only the manner in which she said them. He remembered the stripped and oddly humbled face of Margaret Twining; he looked down at Sarah, poised, wary, inimical, and had a moment of incredulity. This girl had been engaged to Nick, was at least partially convinced that his death was a planned and private thing. She had just heard the news of another murder; she had been shaken for an instant and now had slid deliberately past it, busy with the building of fresh barriers.

And this was the girl who was withholding Nick's letters, and the postcard that contained the last words he had ever written.

Sarah stood up calmly. She held an unlighted cigarette between her fingers and was looking expressionlessly for a match. Sentry forgot his own grim resolutions in a sudden angry desire to seize her and shake her until her composure toppled. When

Sarah took an unhurried step past him he turned and caught her shoulders and brought her sharply around to face him.

Sarah drew in her breath, but that was all. She stood white and unresisting in his hard grip, as though an act of violence had been inevitable between them and she had somehow been prepared for it. Sentry, who had had a coiled whip of words in his mind a split second ago, found that it had vanished, that for a confused moment his senses were fully occupied by the touch of her skin under his hands. Her shoulders were bare and warm and delicately strong, and not what he had meant to be thinking about. Her mouth was very near his. Sentry tightened his hands and bent his head and kissed her without hurry.

He had intended it to be careless, a statement of insulting knowledge; instantly it was something different. There was no time for astonishment; for a blurred and bewildered interval there was no time at all.

Sarah moved, violently, and Sentry dropped his hands and stared at her whitened face, at the mouth that had felt dizzyingly new and disturbingly familiar. Sarah met his eyes directly; her own were wide and steady and unreadable. She said, "It's all right, Andrew. I won't scream."

He had been betrayed, and she had remained untouched; there must be amusement behind that clear pallor. Sentry said coolly, "That's right—you don't, do you?" and watched her take a swift involuntary backward step. They were standing that way, watchful, angry, remembering, when the buzzer sounded.

It startled them both—the classic interruption; it was as though the air between them should have been allowed time to clear. The buzzer sounded again and Sarah went to answer the door.

The edge of the archway into the foyer hid her as she opened it. Then a man's voice said, "I couldn't take the Herberts any longer. Incidentally, why has nobody stuffed the Herberts? Wild Bores, habitat Central Park West. Oh Lord, have I interrupted something?"

They entered the living room, the man tall and languidly amiable, Sarah erect and somehow dauntless. As Sentry came forward from the hearth she said with no cordiality at all, "Mr. Sentry . . . Mr. Court. Andrew is Nick Sentry's brother, James."

Had James Court known that as soon as he stepped into the room? Sentry couldn't be sure. His mind had unravelled six years in an eyelash of time, had raced back to the present again through astonishment and anger and a kind of sick wonder at himself for the shaken feeling that still lingered along his nerves.

Because his errand here was what it was, he made himself shake hands quite casually with the man who had been kissing Sarah Devany in her bedroom on the day he had come to tell her that Nick was dead.

◈ 9

SOMEONE CLOSE TO Sarah Devany, someone who had been in a Japanese prison camp, someone who had known about the approaching interview with Twining . . .

James Court's qualifications were perfect.

Too perfect, Sentry thought, warning away a sudden cold tightening. Too pat, and yet—what better way for Sands to test his immunity? Sentry had had only a lightning glimpse of Court six years ago, but the lazy half-mocking voice was the same, and the idle, almost languid stance with the suggestion of enormous power behind it. Prematurely graying men in horn rims might ordinarily be suspect; Court gave an impression of playing amusedly with the role.

He measured Sentry with frank interest when they shook hands. "You know, I almost looked you up back in '45, after I heard about Nick. Got as far as your house, in fact, but somebody was ill and it didn't seem like a good time for total strangers to be wading in. So I let it go, and you know how those things are . . ."

Sentry nodded, knowing too that Court could have found out from that visit to Barrow Street that it was safe to send a messenger for the prison-camp notebook. "Sarah said you ran into Nick at Cabanatuan."

"I did. Weird, the things that happen in a war. After they broke up O'Donnell—— Look," said Court, interrupting himself, "are you free for dinner? Why don't you join us? Persuade him, Sarah."

Even through his wariness Sentry felt a sardonic amusement at that. He risked a glance at Sarah, sitting quietly on an arm of the couch. She had apparently regained her composure, or was it the braced and desperate nonchalance commonly used for walking past savage dogs? Whatever it was, her unruffled, unruffleable air was back. Sentry felt a reluctant admiration for the calm look she gave him, the cool lift of the dark brows with their delicate crook, the serenity with which she said, "Oh, I've been counting on it. You will, won't you, Andrew?"

Court had seemingly not recognized him as the intruder in Sarah's bedroom at that long-ago cocktail party. Sentry puzzled over that until they were in the restaurant and Court had picked up a wine list to hold it frowningly close. Ah, said Sentry to himself, knowing it was the wholehearted malice of a small boy; Sarah's suitor is as blind as a bat.

They ordered cocktails and dinner and Court, still frowning over the wine list, went into a long and solemn discussion with the headwaiter. He had insisted smilingly on the aisle seat; Sentry was beside Sarah against a mirrored wall. She had put on a shawl that was no more than a web of lacy purple wool. Sentry, extending an automatic hand when she unpinned it, thought she stiffened for a second under the unavoidable touch of his fingers.

How had she explained him to James Court after that broken-into embrace six years ago? Obviously not in his true relationship—unless Court were a remarkable actor. The only recognition in his face had been the same as that in Charles Farrar's, a startled awareness of his resemblance to Nick.

Sands would be startled at what might look for an instant like a dead man's face.

Careful, thought Sentry, tightening again.

◈ 82

The debate with the headwaiter was finally concluded. Cocktails arrived. Court raised his glass to Sentry, said amiably, "Success," and drank. He said reminiscently, "If that wasn't the damnedest thing, finding Nick at Cabanatuan——" and broke off with an uncertain glance at Sarah.

"It's all right," said Sarah steadily. "Really, James. I'm interested too, you know."

Court moved his silver around, made a shining little pile of spoons and separated them again. He said slowly, "Let's see. O'Donnell broke up in—was it July of '42? Around then. They left some doctors behind, and some other prisoners, including me. Before fall of that year they cleared us all out. I was sent . . ."

Sentry, listening, aware of Sarah rigid beside him, had a sudden feeling of helplessness. James Court named places and dates, and they were all, as far as he was concerned, uncheckable. It wasn't vital in any case because Sands, whatever his actual identity, had had ample time in which to piece together an authentic-sounding Army history. It was perfectly possible that he had spent over three years the way Court said he had spent them: on work details in outlying camps.

"That was the hell of it," Court said suddenly. "Where you get a whole prisonful of Americans, you get at least hope—and rumors. There weren't enough of us to concoct a thimble's worth of hope, and the only rumors we got were of our probable demise, any day.

"Eventually they sent us to Cabanatuan—the second week of December, '44. There'd been an outbreak of diphtheria in the camp and nothing to combat it with—a man would have a sore throat one evening and they'd bury him two days later. Nick had gotten it, as a matter of fact, but he was one of the luck——" Court was shocked, too late.

Sentry said nothing, thinking that Nick had been spared from that, too. Spared for Sands. Beside him, Sarah was very still. Court's voice resumed again, but it was determinedly casual now, trying to cover his own ironic echo.

"I didn't know Nick at first." (But Sands had, Sentry reminded himself. Sands had known, and had effaced himself instantly behind a borrowed name and an intentionally blurred background.) "I'd only met him once—you remember, Sarah, up at your family's in Swannet—and of course there'd been," Court paused fleetingly, "changes. I never did get a chance to really talk to him—he was on a railroad detail then and I was put into the hospital on the other side of the compound. It might have been miles away for all the contact we had with the rest of the camp. There'd been rumors that our lot was going on to Japan. We never did, of course, I was still in the hospital when the Rangers came in. But at the time Nick thought I was apt to get home first and, as you know," the light eyes behind the horn-rimmed glasses were on Sarah now, "he asked me to look you up and tell you it wouldn't be long."

And he had delivered the message to Sarah, thought Sentry, and they had gone into each other's arms without heed for the ragged half-starved man who was building his life on his love, who had a plan, who said hopefully that it wouldn't be long.

Sarah turned her head sharply, and he found himself looking into the clear gray eyes. Her lips were a little parted and she had caught a quick small breath as though she were on the verge of speaking.

Here it comes, thought Sentry grimly, the it-was-bigger-than-we-were, we-couldn't-help-ourselves routine. He waited, and saw the intentness go out of her face. In almost the same instant he turned back to James Court, in time to see the curiously pale gaze behind the horn rims remove itself rapidly. They had all

◆ 84

been expecting it, then, Sarah's announcement that she had made a mistake, that if Nick had been there to tell she would have told him first.

Sentry drew a long breath. Court said almost absently, "I had no idea, of course, that Nick was planning a break. It was only a few weeks afterwards that we were liberated. But nobody could chart that. After a while you even stopped expecting it."

Sentry made his voice casual. "Do you remember any of the other men in Nick's barracks?"

Court shook his head reflectively. "I wasn't hitting on all cylinders, of course. Funny, I did think I recognized a fellow I saw only the other day. It was at a country club in Connecticut —I forget the name of the place. But I spoke to him and he didn't know me from Adam, so I must have been wrong."

It was Sentry's turn to move the silver, examining the pattern idly, hiding his sudden shock. The man was undoubtedly Gerald Lyons, at the Shoreline Club. Had the meeting actually happened that way? Or had Court sought Lyons out deliberately, to test his new identity? Sentry singled out a phrase and looked at it again: 'He didn't know me from Adam.' It could be exactly what it seemed, the million-and-first mistake in identity after the war. And it could be a flat and open challenge from Sands.

Sentry lighted a cigarette with care. He said, "Then you don't recall Twining, or a man named Sands?"

"—Sands? I don't think so." Court's long face woke out of thought, was suddenly alert. "I don't remember Twining, either, although maybe if I saw him . . . Sarah's told me something about all this, you know. It must be a hellish thing to have to wonder about. I only wish there were something I could add that would help. Did Twining . . . ?"

"Twining's dead," Sentry told him briefly. He was so weary of waiting for reaction to this particular news that he was startled when James Court's fork stopped in mid-air.

"Dead? Really? And after getting through prison camp . . . what'd he do, slip in the bathtub?"

Sentry shook his head. Sarah Devany said clearly, "Andrew thinks he was murdered."

In the small silence following that a woman at the next table stopped speaking and turned her head to stare piercingly at Sarah. Sentry, who would have preferred to pick his own time, eyed James Court.

Court looked polite and newly interested. "Really? You mean because he—what's the saying—he knew too much? But that would be rather foolish, wouldn't it, because there were other men in camp and he can't have kept a thing like this entirely to himself. I should think it would be much simpler and quicker to kill you off, if that's the object. Stop it at the source, so to speak."

And that, thought Sentry, makes it unanimous. He said "Thanks," dryly. "I'm not keeping any more midnight appointments in the Park."

"I wouldn't in your place," said Court with feeling.

"James," said Sarah in a voice that rose too quickly, "do you think you could commandeer some water?"

Sentry watched them, wondering about a relationship that apparently hadn't ripened to the expected conclusion during six long years. Sarah wore no ring and no radiance; Court was attentive and nothing more.

A beautiful friendship like that, blighted, withered, cooked. Too bad, thought Sentry ironically; a damn shame. Nevertheless he went on wondering, through coffee and the taxi ride downtown and the nightcap Court suggested at a small quiet bar on Twelfth Street.

Sarah refused a drink; Sentry glancing at her, caught the same white, almost forlorn look she had had that first evening when she entered her apartment and found him there. When Court had gone across the small room to greet a gloomy-looking couple in a booth Sentry said quietly, "You didn't happen to find those letters of Nick's, did you, Sarah?"

She shook her head mutely. The hand nearest him on the bar tightened around her gloves.

"But you can see how important they are."

"Yes," Sarah said. "Oh yes, I see that. But I don't——" She broke off, stubbornly silent.

"You don't what?" And what did she need in the way of convincing?

"Nothing," said Sarah abruptly.

And Court came back.

Sentry turned his seething stare on his drink. This was Monday night, and chances were he wouldn't get another opportunity alone with Sarah before she left New York on vacation. She had said Wednesday; that gave him only Tuesday in which to battle her cool, implacable opposition. He was more convinced than ever that there was a name, or a clue to a name or a related thing, among the letters or in the message on the last postcard Nick had ever written. For one thing, he had sent the postcard to Sarah instead of to his father, which had seemed faintly surprising even then. But Sarah would know people Christopher Sentry had never heard of, Sarah might recognize a coded allusion . . .

Meanwhile, he could at least ask the thing that had been vaguely at the back of his mind ever since they had left her apartment. He said casually, "You mentioned Swannet, didn't you? A friend of mine has a place up there—Cy Stevenson. Maybe you've run across him."

He would have said, four days ago, that he trusted Cy Stevenson more than anyone else on earth. Now he was a man moving cautiously through a tunnel, unable to see anything but the faceless figure of Sands at the other end. Until he reached Sands, no one else could really exist. He waited.

"Stevenson?" Sarah said. Her voice was cool, and Sentry wondered whether he had imagined the exploring quality of the quick glance she gave him. "Probably, but it's years since I've spent any time there. I think I've heard my aunt talk about someone named Stevenson."

Sentry nodded gently at her. "That would be your Aunt Harriet?"

She didn't flush. She said crisply, "The very one," and turned her head. "Drink that inch, will you, James, so we can go?"

It was nearly eleven when Sentry reached his apartment and the telephone. He and James Court had left Sarah at her door. At the corner of Eleventh Street Court had paused to say he thought he would go on and meet some friends at the Fifth Avenue; would Sentry care to join him? Sentry, polite over impatience, would not.

He had left his living room windows open and the first slow heavy drops of what felt like an approaching storm were splashing on the sill. Sentry didn't wait to close the windows. He put in a long-distance call and listened to the hollow clickings as it went through, turning a cigarette end over end in nervous fingers. There seemed to be interference on the line; in desperation, he lighted the cigarette. Then a faraway feminine voice was answering: "Shoreline Club."

"Mr. Lyons, please."

"You mean Mr. Lyons in the office?"

"Yes. It's important, so would you——"

A smothered sound at the other end of the wire stopped him. The sound emerged into words. "I'm sorry, but Mr. Lyons is no longer with us."

The raindrops advanced, made a small darkening arc on the rug. Sentry's cigarette flattened between his fingers. He heard his own voice saying nakedly, "What happened?"

There was a pause and then the inarticulate sound again; he realized with sudden damp relief that it was laughter. He said, "It's all right, I'm a friend of his," and the girl sobered and made an attempt to be brisk.

"It was the Donnybrook Fair," she said, still dimly struggling with her own amusement. "And the goats . . . Anyway, Colonel Pembroke—he owns the club—didn't think that Mr. Lyons was —was trying."

And that, temporarily at least, was that. The departing Lyons hadn't left an address or any indication of his plans behind him. Check with Mrs. Lyons tomorrow, thought Sentry, but the ex-assistant manager of the Shoreline Club hadn't seemed like a man who would trot repentantly back home.

It would be interesting indeed to find out if a tall languid man in horn-rims actually had turned up to greet Lyons by name at the Shoreline Club.

Meanwhile there was something else, some small and persistently weaving thread that he had caught hold of once during the evening and released too soon. He had felt then, he felt now that if he could trace it to its end it would turn out to be important.

Cunningly, Sentry put his attention elsewhere.

Sarah Devany stared for a long moment at the closet door in her bedroom, firmly closed now although she had left it open in her anxiety not to leave James Court and Andrew Sentry alone together too long.

Her bedroom windows were up, and the lifting wind that preceded the storm might have blown the door shut. But it couldn't have turned the stiff doorknob, and you had to do that to make the thing stay closed.

There had been someone here while she was out, someone who had carefully and too mechanically restored order behind him.

Sarah was suddenly and blazingly angry. She went across the room and flung the closet door open, over a last-minute quake of fright, and looked in at ranked and orderly clothes. She went next to the desk in the living room, and saw proof again of a disturbing hand; bills she had meant to pay tonight were at the bottom of the sheaf.

A scatter of hollow puncturing sounds made her whirl. The rain had begun in a fat lazy handful of drops that quickened almost instantly to a downpour. Ten minutes later, by the time Sarah had followed approximately the path of the unknown searcher, the apartment was echoing with drum-rolls of thunder.

She closed the windows against brilliant lightning and realized that, half-consciously, she had been expecting something like this silent invasion. Andrew Sentry had known she was lying about Nick's letters—and Andrew had closed the door of her apartment earlier this evening when they had all gone out to dinner. Or, perhaps, not quite closed it? It would have been simple enough for him to signal to someone as they left the building.

He hadn't found what he came for, she thought. Unless—a peal of thunder, wincingly close, cut off the rest of the half-formed thought. When the sound had died into a long flicker of lightning she had forgotten everything but her own cold steady anger. That Andrew should have commissioned a friend—or weren't there people who conducted searches of this kind professionally?—to rifle her possessions and shatter her small area of privacy was all at once intolerable.

She could at least let him know that his emissary had betrayed him. Sarah crossed the living room to the phone, found that she had to look up his number and dialled it violently. The line was busy.

The apartment seemed very still when she put back the receiver. Very still and somehow waiting, as though the alien presence that had possessed it briefly had left a vague and hovering impress there. Nonsense, thought Sarah briskly, and even said it aloud.

It was only that the windows, which she had closed at the height of the storm, needed opening. She did that briskly too, and came back to light every lamp in the living room and smoke a cigarette while she waited for Andrew Sentry's line to be free.

The terror began gently and quietly. At first it was one of the bedroom blinds clicking in a pour of rainy air, and then it was the hypnotizing sense of her own immobility and her foolishly pounding heart. She became aware rigidly, listeningly, of just how accessible a ground-floor apartment was. She paused frozenly in the act of lifting her forgotten cigarette, and discovered that the slender shape of darkness crawling across the rug had been the shadow of her moving wrist.

And then the terror sprang, with a sequence of thoughts so soft and clear that they might have been delivered in her ear by human lips.

Suppose the presence in her apartment had nothing to do with Andrew Sentry at all.

◈ *91*

Suppose it was somehow a part of the bitterly reminding mystery that had come to light after six bleak years.

Suppose it had been the man who called himself Sands.

Sarah moved, under the impact of a new and different fear. The quiet round-faced clock on the mantel said eleven-thirty, but Jane would still be up; Jane, night-watchman of security for uncounted years. Even the memory of Jane's brown aquiline face and short curly white hair and milky blue eyes was oddly comforting.

"Long-Distance?" said Sarah at the phone, and was inordinately fond of the voice that answered, impersonal though it was. "I'd like to put in a person-to-person call to Swannet, Massachusetts . . ."

Sands was within a few years either way of Sentry's own age, thirty-five.

He was either a native or a long-resident New Yorker.

He was an educated man, possibly from a wealthy background.

He was dark. (Then.)

He was notably fastidious.

He barked when he laughed—or was it only pre-murder nerves?

He was almost certainly either a friend of Sarah Devany's or someone whom Nick had met in his own specialized line of work, as otherwise chances were that Sentry would have known him too.

And from the foregoing facts, not perhaps conclusive when taken singly, said Sentry bitterly to himself, I deduce not a damn thing.

But there was something, somewhere, and it was as irritating as though he had trudged miles to a store and, arriving, had forgotten what he came for. Something that had been said casually by either Sarah or the elegant Mr. Court. Sentry worried discontentedly at it for a time and then went resignedly to bed.

He was at the edge of sleep when it came mockingly to wake him. It was the recurring reference to the town of Swannet, by Cy, by Megan, by James Court and Sarah Devany. Sarah's relatives were there, of course, but Nick had been there, too, at least once, on the occasion when he and Court had met.

Nick had been there, among that small closed circle of people who, two days ago, had known or could have been informed of Sentry's projected visit to Robert Twining . . .

Sentry lay in darkness, examining that.

So there were two common denominators—Sarah Devany, and a small Massachusetts town. Of the two, Swannet was a blind spot, the only complete blank, Sentry realized with a new alertness, in his knowledge of Nick. Was Swannet more than the original meeting ground of all these people—was Swannet the heart of the web? Had the Devanys in some way played a part——

But not the Devanys; the family name was something else. Thoroughly awake, Sentry got out of bed and went into the darkened living room and switched on the lamp near the bookcase. On his removal from the Barrow Street house he had brought, among other books from the library, his father's complete set of Trollope, one of Christopher Sentry's most fondly regarded collections. He had had even at the time a vivid memory of his father's last Christmas, of Christopher unwrapping a day-late present and lifting out a calf volume with sudden warm pleasure. "Orley Farm! Well, that does it, I've got them all now. Lord—it's from Sarah's aunt. I call that handsome, seeing we've never laid eyes on each other."

Sarah's aunt, thought Sentry now. But had she . . . ? Yes, she had. It was there on the flyleaf, decisive and black, at the bottom of a brief message he didn't bother to read.

". . . Jane Trellishaw."

Pavick, perplexed and perplexing "—and then something about a trellis."

Trellis . . .

. . . Trellishaw.

10

"COME IN," said Miss Augusta Glass briskly. "I take it you're Mr. Sentry?"

Sentry said that he was, and unobtrusively offered the driver's license he hadn't used in four years. Miss Glass, murmuring politely that it was not at all necessary, craned forward across her desk for a sharp look at it.

Cy Stevenson's aunt was a tall woman in her early sixties with short curly gray hair, pouched and cynical eyes and the complexion of a well-exposed shingle. The desk she sat at was a miracle of disorder, with only the tip of an inkstand pen emerging from a welter of correspondence, photographs of houses, and mimeographed folios in clips. As Sentry watched a telephone rang and Miss Glass thrust a hand unerringly into the debris, lifted out a receiver, listened a moment and then began to address it with savage gusto.

Sentry turned away to examine the photographed houses tacked on a burlap board. It had been startlingly easy to leave New York after his years of tenure—a matter of telephoning Cy, packing a bag and locking the apartment behind him. It had been startlingly easy too to take Lucy Allard to a farewell lunch at the Biltmore, although neither of them had called it that. He had wondered for the last few weeks whether he was in love with Lucy; when she met him under the clock, with the usual collection of involuntary glances following her, he had known illogically and with a vast relief that he was not.

The certainty helped, because now his existence started clean and cold from the night he had found out about Nick's murder.

Miss Glass concluded her conversation, lifted out the telephone and shepherded a number of stray papers under it. She stood up, taking a key from the center desk drawer. "I close in half an hour anyway, Mr. Sentry, so if you'd like I'll show you the way to the cottage. Swannet isn't an easy town to find your way around in."

She paused to lock the door of the shop under the black-lettered sign that said, "Augusta Glass, Inc., Real Estate," surveyed the curb, and said, "Shall we take my car? Some fool has sewed me up here, but I think I can wriggle out."

"Perhaps if I got out first," said Sentry, abashed, and slid into his rented car to wait with the motor idling while Miss Glass maneuvered her old Chevrolet into the traffic on Commercial Street. Ten minutes later, half a mile beyond the center of the little town, he followed her up a short steep hill, pulled to a stop and got out of the car to join her on the edge of what had once been lawn and was now tall reddish grass.

"Here it is," said Miss Glass reverently. "There's a cove down under those rocks in back where you can swim. I could get the moon for this place on a summer rental if Cy weren't so stubborn."

The cottage was very small and white, its door and shutters faded apple green. Perched on a table of rock against a purpling sky, it looked like an extravagant playhouse for children. Inside the tiny living room Miss Glass looked at Sentry measuringly and said briskly, "You'll have to do a bit of stooping through doorways, I'm afraid."

Ducking obediently, Sentry followed her through the miniature first floor. In spite of its size, the cottage bore the air of a roomy old farmhouse looked at through a reducing glass: white-washed walls, floors painted green-gray, door hinges and living room fireplace painted black. At one side of the hearth was a pygmy staircase leading up; at the other, folds of chintz parted on a bedroom. The bathroom opened off a kitchen no larger than a ship's galley but surprisingly complete for its size, with shelves, sink, refrigerator and hot plate.

Back in the living room, Miss Glass waved a hand at the ceiling. "There's a bedroom and lavatory upstairs, although I don't know whether Cy's kept it equipped. It has a simply marvelous view of the water, in case you prefer sleeping upstairs . . . I think that's all. Will you leave the key with me when you go?"

Sentry said he would, expressed his thanks and went down with her to her car. A mist was blowing in from the sea; it gave the roofs and hills and tree-tops of the town below them a gauzy watercolor look. Sentry said blandly, holding the door for Miss Glass, "I'm pretty well lost anywhere north of the Bronx River Parkway, but don't the Trellishaws live somewhere around here?"

Miss Glass gave him a sharp look out of the pouched eyes. "Yes, they do. They're about two miles away from here by road, but it's not even three-quarters of a mile over the hill. Jane Trellishaw is a good friend of mine. Cy's met the family, I believe he even saw something of—— I hope you'll enjoy the cottage, Mr. Sentry."

Inside again, Sentry found lights and unpacked his single bag in the first floor bedroom. The bottle of bourbon he put on the bureau; the Colt .45 he had bought just before his discharge from the Army he held in his hands gently, tentatively, the way he had balanced it that morning in his New York apartment. He turned it carefully in his fingers, knowing that in spite of four years of war a gun had never felt quite like this in his hands before. Then he put the Colt in a bureau drawer, carried the bourbon into the kitchen, made a small drink so that the bottle should look friendlier when he got back, locked the front door behind him and went down to his car.

There was one market still open on Commercial Street. Sentry bought milk, eggs, bacon, butter, bread, cheese, coffee, sugar, some canned meat and a quantity of soups. The pretty dark-haired girl at the cashier's counter said, "My. Looks like you're laying in for a siege."

"It does, doesn't it?" said Sentry.

He found the cottage again after one wrong turning, and was pleasantly surprised at the way its lights flowed down over the rock and the neglected lawn and the swimming waist-high mist. The sound of the waves was very clear; he listened to it while he had another leisurely drink, two cheese sandwiches that tasted odd until he realized that he had forgotten to buy mustard, and coffee. There was wood in a kind of Dutch oven beside the fireplace. Sentry built a fire, sat down in a large and ramshackle armchair that was obviously of Cy's choosing and knew that in spite of his own carefully detached and casual actions, his determination to watch and wait before making his next move, his hatred had gained upon him strongly ever since he had entered this house.

Was it because the Trellishaws' house lay not quite three-quarters of a mile over the hill—because he was close now to whatever had lain behind Nick's murder? Sentry went on listening moodily to the muted rush of waves in the cove behind the cottage; the sound was somehow infinitely discouraging. Water over the dam—too much of it? Sands had been connected somehow with the Trellishaw family; Nick had died because he knew the enormity of that connection. And yet—how many years ago? While Sands went free, while Nick himself said nothing until that night outside a prison camp in the Philippines?

Time, thought Sentry, operated against him in two ways: the vanished years since Nick had been murdered, the capsuled summer when he and Nick, both reserve officers, had been called into the Army within two months of each other.

That's it, thought Sentry, and the sudden clear certainty woke him out of the half-drowse of the firelight on the walls and the distant sound of the sea. That's when it happened.

Carefully, now; go back. To early July, 1941, and the night Nick had brought Sarah back to the house on Barrow Street, and Sarah had had a look of floating on Nick's arm, of not being moored to the ground at all. A child would have known what had happened to them, but half their delight now was their new shyness in the presence of a third. Sentry remembered descending the stairs again in their speechless faces and saying resignedly, "Always a best man and never a bride. Is that champagne under your arm, Nick? If it isn't it ought to be . . ."

They had had the champagne and Sarah had said lazily, happily, "Nick dear, you'll have to go up and meet my family. And certify your intentions, I mean—we're a very proper lot, and you needn't think you can trifle. It's north of Boston—did you know there was anything north of Boston?"

Sentry's orders had arrived a week after that and he had reported to a southern camp. And Nick had gone on an unknown date to the Trellishaws' in Swannet, at which time—it seemed almost certain—Sands had "gotten away with something."

That he had gotten away with something was the solid rooftree in Sentry's house of shadows; Nick himself had said as much in that fatal accusation outside the barracks at Cabanatuan. That it had happened here in Swannet followed for Sentry as the night the day: "trellis" had a fairly low frequency in the language, and Trellishaw was a far from common name.

He combed the red remaining coals of the fire under the ashes

◈ 99

and went to bed, to lie smoking in the unfamiliar dark. He put out his cigarette at last, and his mind resumed its sinister play of the night before. A child's game, to catch a killer—the holding up of various personalities, like paper cutouts, against the basic figure of Sands.

The figure was dim, but he had caught it in two definite actions: the commandeering of Nick's prison camp notebook and the sudden destruction of Robert Twining. There should have been grounds for conjecture in how the people concerned had occupied that Saturday evening, but his circuitous questions in every case had produced nothing.

Cy Stevenson, for instance, had volunteered a giant quarrel with the girl he had taken out, after which he had, he said, gone on a sulky tour of all the bars between Central Park and Washington Square. James Court had rushed Sarah Devany through an early dinner; there were distant relatives from the West to be met at LaGuardia Field and shown a judicious part of town. Farrar had broken an engagement with Megan in order to entertain one of his law firm's more prominent clients at a soothingly dull midtown club. None of it checkable, and yet . . .

Cy Stevenson, whose cottage he now occupied, who had said that morning with evident relief, "Now you're talking. The place is going begging, and you could certainly use a rest. If you took it easy for a couple of weeks things might shake down . . . I'll call my Aunt Augusta before you change your mind, and tell her you're picking up the key."

Cy was a little big for Sands, thought Sentry coldly, but Sands might have been down to half his weight at Cabanatuan. According to his own account, Cy had gone from Camp O'Donnell back to Bilibid—but it would take months of writing to Washington to prove that. And if there were a juggled name concerned, what then? There was no place now for the persistent feeling of shame because it was Cy who had watched him through nightmare, Cy who had been awkward and embarrassed and as gentle as a woman, who had stayed up with him through incoherent nights and dreamlike days. Had Cy ever mentioned the Trellishaws? Sentry's own recognition of the name was so new that he couldn't be sure. And yet Augusta Glass had mentioned them, and had broken off sharply on the brink of something else.

There was James Court, the elegantly grayed Mr. Court, whose faint air of aloof amusement might fit the fastidiousness ascribed to Sands. Sentry lay quietly, concentratingly in darkness and remembered his first impression of Court, an impression of enormous power behind a deliberately languid pose. Sands had been dark at Cabanatuan, but dark hair had been known to turn quite rapidly under shock and tension.

All right; Farrar. Find out where Farrar had spent the war years, find out, if possible, more about his reported nervous breakdown. Discard, certainly, the scrubbed and earnest look, the almost childish anxiety to do the proper, the gentlemanly thing. Farrar, as Megan Ware's fiancé, was closer to the Trellishaws than either Cy or Court—and Sarah had said last night, "They're engaged again." Again . . . had there been a ring before or merely an understanding? Look into that, look into all of it.

Because, unless Sentry's intent with regard to Twining had been communicated by thought transference, unless any number of illogical and far-fetched things, one of these men was Sands. One of them had watched Nick's execution by Japanese soldiers, one of them had maneuvered Robert Twining cleverly, fatally into the path of an onrushing car.

Had it been Sands who toasted him mockingly in the restaurant with Sarah? Sands who mixed him a drink while he waited in Sarah's apartment on that first night of raw new knowledge? Or Sands who had lent him this cottage, who had slept in this very bed?

Sentry lay quiet, sweating in the cool darkness. After a while the blind angry hurry of his heartbeats slowed, but it was a long time before he slept.

"Mr. Sentry?" said Jane Trellishaw's clipped, rather deep voice. "Oh, of course—you're Nick's . . . you're Andrew. How nice of you to phone."

Sentry, squeezed into a drug store phone booth, thought that her voice sounded pleasant. He said, listening cautiously to his own lie, "I've heard Sarah speak of you so often that I hoped you wouldn't mind. What I really called for this morning was to offer transportation—I knew Sarah was planning to come up from New York today and I'd be glad to drive into Boston for her if it would save anybody a trip."

Sarah had apparently never confided in her aunt; Jane Trellishaw sounded only innocently grateful. "Thanks so much, Mr. Sentry, but as a matter of fact Sarah and Charles—Mr. Farrar, you know, my other niece's fiancé—are driving up together." She paused, and to Sentry's amusement added politely, "I imagine that with Sarah here on vacation we'll be seeing you soon in any case."

"I hope so. As a matter of fact," said Sentry, leaping hastily at a door of welcome that seemed to be closing gradually but firmly, "would you mind if I dropped around for a few minutes some time this morning? I'd like to talk to you, if it wouldn't be interrupting something."

"Of course not, we'd be delighted." The reply was warm and instant; bewilderment was there only if you looked for it. Finding it, Sentry swallowed his own distaste and said firmly, "You people saw Nick after I did, you know. There are one or two questions . . ."

"Of course," said Sarah's aunt again, and this time the reserve was plain. She had apparently, thought Sentry grimly, hanging up after they had agreed upon an hour's time, no more liking than he for the harrowing rehash of the dead, the unreeling of last words and final gestures, the busy, futile raking of the ashes.

But it had worked. He would find out from her when Nick had visited the Trellishaws and he would gain access to the house and at least one of the people in it before Sarah could arrive and build a wall of hostility against him. And with the date of Nick's coming established, there would be the local papers for that time, the local gossip . . .

Meanwhile there was still the best part of an hour to kill. Sentry spent it driving around the small harbor town, thronged now with summer people and tourists. He found lobster traps piled up in front of old and unexpectedly beautiful houses, and ancient rowboats drawn up on tiny velvet lawns. He stopped once at a pond set serenely into the cap of a hill; beyond it, like a stage set, wine-glass elms towered over the summerhouse of a hillside cemetery. An old man basking on a stone bench caught Sentry's arrested gaze, nodded at the pond, said, "Ain't no bottom to it," and spat proudly.

There were flowers everywhere, tumbling out of window-boxes, tendrilling among the fences. There were innumerable artists perched on camp chairs, soberly perpetuating hollyhocks and house-fronts. There was, over everything, the blanched and stinging August sunlight thrown back from sand and rocks and water. Sentry, who had looked forward to a bored and aimless hour, found that he was late and turned his car reluctantly away from the harbor and its snowflake sailboats.

◆ *103*

He knew the house at once from Jane Trellishaw's description: "A yellow Cape Cod, next to the greenhouse on your left—there are two maples in the yard." It was a very pale yellow, lemony, with white shutters and two stone chimneys. The maples had an odd fountaining shape. Sentry got out of his car, walked through the narrow opening in a privet hedge, and was on his way up the irregular stone path when he saw a woman coming toward him around the side of the house. She had short white hair and a brown aquiline face, a flat lean body in faded blue jeans and a basque shirt. She carried a trowel in one gloved hand. She said in the cool and rather deep voice he had heard on the telephone, "I'm Jane Trellishaw. Did you have any trouble finding us?"

That and his answer got them inside the house, dim after the brilliant morning. Sarah's aunt led Sentry into a small informal living room full of cool muted colors. She said briskly, "Megan and her mother are out shopping, I know they'll be sorry to have missed you this time, Mr. Sentry. I usually have some iced coffee about now—can I get you a glass?"

She was gone, and the door she had closed unobtrusively behind her moved gently open a little way. Sentry got up silently and crossed the floor and looked into another larger living room, making an L to the one he stood in. The door was cooperative; it swung wider without a sound. The inner room was long, with a blue-painted floor and flowered curtains at the windows, armchairs and small tables, a fireplace, a spinet desk. There was a photograph on the desk.

Sentry paused, heard the rush of water and the clink of an ice tray somewhere in the hidden distance and went quietly over to the desk. A blond and poker-faced child of—what, twelve? thirteen?—looked at him out of the narrow silver frame. Megan Ware, obviously, in a dress with a wide lace collar;

Megan before she had learned about being little-girlish. There was another child at her shoulder, taller and plainly older, who managed somehow to look gay in spite of a severe Dutch bob and a hint of what must be braces on her teeth. The hair was dark, the eyes light.

Sarah? With braces on her teeth? Sentry found the possibility very satisfying; it was undermining to Sarah's cool and immaculate air. There was certainly something hauntingly familiar about the dark gay child. Sentry stood in front of the photograph, lips pursed in a soundless whistle, and then, as the refrigerator door echoed somewhere beyond him, went rapidly and noiselessly out of the room. When Jane Trellishaw reappeared in the little gray-green living room with two glasses of iced coffee he had a cigarette in his fingers and was going industriously through his pockets for a match.

Sarah's aunt sat down in a small toile-covered slipper chair. She had obviously braced herself for reminiscence if Sentry wanted it; she said, examining him coolly, "Lord, don't you look like Nick!"

Sentry was ready for that; he said easily, "We've been taken for twins. I hope this isn't breaking up your morning, by the way. Cigarette?"

"I'd love one."

Sentry crossed the room and lighted it; it occurred to him briefly in transit that men had a parallel to woman's intuition—the knowledge of being measured for a husband. Sarah's aunt was doing just that behind her narrow brown likable face, weighing and judging him as to his fitness for Sarah.

She caught his eye and glanced away, casually. "Sarah and Charles got an early start this morning, incidentally. Charles called a few minutes ago to say they were stopping for an early lunch somewhere in Connecticut."

"I understand he had a bad time of it after the war."

"He did, rather." If Jane Trellishaw were surprised she didn't show it; she went on, "He wasn't in good shape at all when he came East, and the doctors thought he needed a few months of complete rest. So he went out to a place in Phoenix for a while, MacPherson's, I think it was, to forget all about New Guinea."

Sentry nodded and said a friend of his had done the same thing, and came immediately back to the business in hand. "I wouldn't have bothered you about this, you know, except that I got called before Nick did, and I've always wondered——"

"Naturally," said Jane Trellishaw, and met his eyes squarely. "I don't think I need to tell you how shocked we all were, how horrified . . . It's late in the day to be saying this, but there hasn't really been a chance before."

The conversation was going the wrong way; Sentry made appropriate responses and steered it carefully back. "When I left to report for duty I knew Nick was planning to come up here. I never did find out when he made it."

"It was the last week of August," said Jane Trellishaw abruptly. "The week-end. He and Sarah came up Friday night. There was——" She stopped, not looking at Sentry, staring instead at a white spray of rambler roses that hung at one of the windows. Her voice sounded deadened when she went on. "We were all delighted about Sarah and Nick. There was a party that Saturday night—we'd wanted it outside but the heat spell broke late Saturday afternoon and it poured, so we had it here in the house."

Sentry waited quietly, tightly. Was there anything here at all? Or was this only a conscientious scraping-together of trivia, an effort to bridge an unbridgeable gap? Sarah's aunt lifted her gaze from the rug and said with a half-questioning air, "Nick left the party early, you know, at about twelve."

She thought, of course, that Sarah had told him. Sentry said, "Why was that, anyway?"

It was his taxi, Jane Trellishaw explained. Nick had had to be at Logan Airport at a certain time, and the local cab company had called at the last minute to say that there was trouble at the garage and the driver would be late. It wasn't unusual for Swannet on a rainy Saturday night. As she talked, Sentry saw the sequel vividly: Nick, characteristically impatient at waiting, refusing to allow Sarah to dig the Trellishaw car from the crowded driveway, wanting to say his goodbyes quickly and mercifully for them both, without leaving Sarah the lonely wet desolate trip home. And there was a short-cut to the public garage, Jane said.

"Short-cut?" repeated Sentry.

"Yes—over the hill and through the fields. You get down to the harbor that way, and the garage, and save about two miles by road. It's rather rough going if you don't know the way—as a matter of fact Nick lost a cigarette lighter en route. One of the Thatcher boys, they live up on the other side of the pond, brought it back a few weeks later—it had his name on it. It was so rusted and ruined that I didn't even think about trying to return it."

Was she offering him meticulous details in lieu of something else, something much more important? Listening to the carefully off-hand voice, the tiny gestures of brows and hands that went with it, Sentry thought so. He brushed the lighter from the surface of his consciousness, and watched and waited.

Sarah's aunt had paused again, her long candid face remote in some recollection of her own. The effort with which she shook herself out of it was visible. "And—I don't know what else I can tell you, Mr. Sentry. We wanted to make it a good party, of course, because we knew Nick was leaving the next day, and I think everybody guessed it was a port of embarkation. I do think," said Jane Trellishaw, looking for the first time bleak and old, "that it was what people call a good party. At least . . ."

And that was all. She asked him politely if he would have more iced coffee, but there was dismissal in every line of her. Sentry thanked her; they were at the privet hedge when she said abruptly, "Won't you come over for lunch on Saturday, Mr. Sentry? If you're free, that is. It won't be anything formal, we're generally at the beach too much for that. But if you'd like to——"

Sentry said that he would like it very much, and added casually that he was staying just above a beach of sorts himself, at Cy Stevenson's cottage. He wondered if there was a faint re-action to that, if Jane Trellishaw's lashes had flicked startledly over her milky blue eyes. Then she was saying composedly, "That's a very nice little place, as I remember it. Is Cy with you? Well, we'll look forward to seeing you Saturday, Mr. Sentry."

Sentry drove immediately to the public library, a smoky red brick pile on a hill overlooking the harbor. He found, after considerable pulling in and out of drawers, the Swannet *Star* for the last week of August.

He went through it carefully because what he was looking for might be buried on one of the inside pages, might even be an item in the personal or lost and found or real estate columns, might not be there at all. He read about the school opening dates, a town meeting, unending lists of people who would be the guests of other people over the Labor Day week-end. There was no mention at all of the Trellishaws—or of Cy Stevenson or James Court or Charles Farrar.

But it must have been then, thought Sentry blankly; it had to be then.

He reached without hope for the next issue, dated the first Friday in September, and it was there, looking at him from the bottom right-hand corner of the front page. It was headlined "Local Girl is Crash Victim" and under that it said that Eleanora Ware, 23, daughter of Mrs. Howard Trellishaw of Coldpoint Road, had been found dead in her wrecked car early the preceding Sunday morning. The driver of the car, which was registered in Miss Ware's name, was not on the scene and had not come forward for questioning.

The Medical Examiner said that Eleanora Ware had bled to death over a period of hours from injuries sustained in the crash.

11

THE CAR IN WHICH Eleanora Ware was clearly a passenger had failed to negotiate a sharp curve on the road leading out to Sutter's Point and had crashed into a stone parapet over a small stream. It was a notoriously dangerous turn, and the parapet was scarred by other impacts over the years.

The smashed dashboard clock which had apparently been in good running order previous to the accident said 12:16; both the physician at the scene and the Medical Examiner agreed as to the fitness of the indicated time. Eleanora Ware had died at some time between three and four a.m. that Sunday, of shock and loss of blood.

That meant a lapse of roughly three hours. Ample time, thought Sentry, seeing again the dark gay face of Megan Ware's older sister, in which to bleed to death.

He went back once more, unrewardingly, over the nine-year-old story. There were no conclusions drawn or even sketched by the Swannet *Star;* to Sentry, possessed of his own cold knowledge, the inferences were so appalling that he might have been holding a grenade instead of a yellowed corner of newspaper. Jane Trellishaw said out of an echo: "Nick left the party early, you know. At about twelve."

Well, now he knew.

At two o'clock on that brilliantly hot afternoon Sentry presented himself, in accordance with the nurse's advice, at the office of H. Addison Palmer, M.D. Palmer was a big and surprisingly youthful man in an immaculate tan gabardine suit; he had a ruddy face and crisp dark hair, arched black brows over lazily drooping eyes and an air of easy arrogance that Sentry disliked on sight. He looked impetuous and very competent.

He said, cocking a silk ankle up on a languidly extended knee, "Of course I remember the Eleanora Ware case. We don't have many around here like that, thank God. But——" Palmer's eyelids flickered shut under the raised brows, the white teeth were bared in a deprecating smile, "is it, frankly, a concern of yours, Mr. Sentry?"

"Very much so," said Sentry flatly. "You have only my word for that, but I can assure you that it's of the utmost importance."

Palmer stared at him out of bold black eyes, lifted the astonishingly agile brows again and shrugged; his manner said that rather than fritter away his valuable time in arguing with eccentrics he would give in gracefully. He skated his swivel chair backward to a file, pulled out a metal drawer, drew a folder from it and skated nimbly back.

He said shortly, glancing up again at Sentry, "What is it you want to know? What she died of? Well, here's the list—lateral fracture of the skull, compound fracture of——"

"I understand," said Sentry quietly, "that she bled to death."

"Well, she did," said Palmer, still brusque, closing the folder. "That is, if she'd had immediate attention, if that hadn't been such a Godforsaken stretch of road, she'd have lived. She was young and extraordinarily healthy, one of the wiry ones. But nobody with those injuries can crawl around in a smashed-up windshield and then collapse for hours half-out in the rain and get away with it."

Sentry let out his breath very gently. He said, "What about the—driver, Doctor? Wouldn't he have been marked up a bit?"

"No doubt about it. There was blood on the handle of the

driver's door, and more traces down the side where the rain hadn't washed it away," said Palmer. "It looked as though the driver had jumped out while the car was in motion, possibly just before it hit."

"And," said Sentry, depositing a match carefully in the hollowed silver back of a surrealist duck, "they never found any trace of the man?"

"There was never any proof that it was a man," Palmer said curtly, putting away the folder.

Sentry found himself suddenly angry. "Young ladies rarely go out in cars with other young ladies at midnight after a party."

And Palmer capitulated unexpectedly. "Well, you're right, of course. Knowing Eleanora Ware—and apart from that the state of her lipstick—yes, I'd say it was a man and an affectionate one." He leaned forward across the desk, his ruddy face serious. "Look here, Sentry. I don't know what your interest is in all this, but I happen to be the Trellishaws' doctor. They're important people, and they're damn nice people. They don't like this thing hashed over, and I can't say I blame them."

He paused and began to turn a pencil end over end on his desk; Sentry thought detachedly that it must be a gesture taught to every intern as part of a course in How to Win Patients and Look Preoccupied with Bigger Things. He waited.

Palmer said brutally, "Eleanora Ware was as pretty as the devil and just as indiscreet. She wasn't engaged, her younger sister was. Eleanora was the kind of girl that should have been married as soon as the law allows, but she had a Yankee stepfather who thought otherwise. So what if she did take her car out with a few drinks in her and pick up some guy who liked her looks? Suppose he did smash up her car and then take to his heels to keep from getting involved with a stranger? It wouldn't make history, it's been done God knows how many times. The girl's dead, there was never any trace of the man. What can you stir up now but mud?"

It was a strange portrait of a girl, Sentry thought, out on the street again; as strange and startling in this atmosphere as a parrot blazing up in a nest of well-mannered wrens. He considered that for a moment, remembered Megan Ware's calculated demureness, and took it back.

But still—how many families would have accepted Palmer's cynical hypothesis? Unless the taker of that portrait in the Trellishaw living room had been almost clairvoyant, unless the air of defiant gayety about eyes and brows, the promise of recklessness in the curling mouth, had deepened and materialized through the years.

It would explain quite a few things. The abruptness with which the case had been allowed to drop. Jane Trellishaw's frozen look when she had told him of the party for Nick. Sarah Devany's failure to make any connection between two sudden deaths within her own small sphere—because Eleanora Ware's fate had long ago been reasoned out and tucked gracefully away under the label of tragic foolishness.

And it might have been that way, if Nick hadn't said, at Cabanatuan, "How long did you think you'd get away with it?" in relation to the Trellishaws; if Nick hadn't been instantly silenced. If he, Nick's brother, hadn't learned of that prearranged execution and planned to go to Robert Twining for help; if Twining hadn't been fed with reunion drinks and then pushed deliberately into the path of a car.

Sands tended toward cars. He had leaped from behind the wheel of one in the very beginning, and slipped away to leave a young girl bleeding to death. It was, thought Sentry, pausing on the elm-shaded sidewalk to light a cigarette, a peculiarly cold and careless crime, to which there could be no extenuating circumstances whatever. There could certainly have been no alcoholic blank. Split-second reaction had saved Eleanora's companion from possible death; a sharp awareness had memorized Nick's face during what must have been a racing encounter in the dark.

Who had been missing from the party during the interval in question? Sentry realized the hopelessness of that before he even began to attack it. At midnight there would have been people going home, seeing other people to their cars, congregating in the kitchen, vanishing upstairs for raincoats and scarves. Jane Trellishaw, as co-hostess, would have been far too preoccupied to connect times and faces, and Jane was, he thought grimly, the only person in that house whom he could trust.

And how, since——

A horn tootled wheezingly at Sentry. Augusta Glass, in her purplish-black Chevrolet, took one hand off the wheel in a perilous wave as she threaded past him on the narrow hill. Sentry lifted a hand in salute, started his own car and headed back for the cottage.

That was Wednesday. Two more days had to go by before he would see Sarah and Megan Ware and Charles Farrar in their proper context, at the Trellishaw house; before he could find out from Jane Trellishaw details of the party that had brought about one death and planted the small deadly core of another. Sentry found that his own straining urgency had been replaced by a cold singleness of thought that was almost content to wait.

Meanwhile, the town's influx of tourists had reached its peak of the summer, and Sentry's idle amiable questions in drug stores, restaurants and the Swansdown Café produced no animosity at all. A great deal of what he got was interested surmise, but there was at least a background of fact.

The Trellishaws had always been important in the town. At the time they moved there from Maine there had been three of them, Howard, Jane and Elizabeth. Elizabeth had married Thomas Devany and there was a child, Sarah; the Devanys had been drowned in a sailing accident when their daughter was ten.

Two years before the double tragedy, Howard Trellishaw had married Harriet Ware, a widow with two young daughters. The orphaned Sarah was in the course of time taken into her uncle's family and brought up with the Ware girls, Megan and Eleanora.

In 1942, just a year after his elder step-daughter's death in a car crash, Howard Trellishaw had died of pneumonia. His unmarried sister Jane, who had been living for some time with her brother and his family, was made a permanent part of the household under a stipulation in the will. Benevolence, in insuring a home for his sister? Or a police action, setting a watch on the twice-widowed Harriet Ware? Sentry was curious, but it was hardly a question that could be put with nonchalance.

He tried for it by indirection. "Money, wasn't there?"

"And then some. Say," said his informant, with coolness under his geniality for the first time, "what line are you in, anyway? Insurance? Real estate? I thought you said you had a friend who——"

"I did. He was killed in the war, but you know how it is," Sentry said carelessly, "you get interested in people from the little you hear about them. How about another beer? Can't fly on two wings . . ."

It rained Thursday night and most of Friday, a wild windy downpour that turned out later to be the edge of a hurricane.

There was no answer as yet to the night letter Sentry had sent to MacPherson's, Phoenix, Arizona. With the exception of one drenching half-blinded trip into the town Sentry stayed in the cottage, playing the restless game that had come to have an ugly fascination: pinning a face on Sands. Sands, who had begun to kill in this small, salty, oddly gay town. Sands, whose very unsureness had given him confidence to kill twice more.

Had Nick, perhaps, traded cigarettes with Sands, entered with him into the tiny, laughable, deadly serious exchanges of a prison camp? I.O.U. one scoop of rice for two cigarettes; one bone, to pound into powder and sprinkle on rice, for one portion of the cloudy weed-flavored water that was issued as soup.

One life, in exchange for a chance glimpse of something that wouldn't bear looking at, that couldn't be told. Sands had collected. Sands, thought Sentry savagely, had still to be collected from.

The cottage echoed with the lost lonely sound of wind and rain. Water seeped and trickled across the window sills; Sentry diverted himself by making dams of cunningly creased newspaper and found, when he stepped back to inspect them, that he was standing in a lake that had swum under the door. A spread-out shirt from the laundry bag did admirably for five minutes. The laundry bag itself, sausage-rolled with its contents, was better still.

There was no radio, no telephone. Sentry spent Thursday evening combing grimly through the bookcase; as in many summer cottages furnished hastily, handsome bindings opened up on plane geometry, *The New Scholasticism*, Burton's *Anatomy of Melancholy*. Sentry settled down morosely with Volume III of Smollett between marbled covers and found his mind straying to Sarah Devany.

Sarah, orphaned at the age of ten, set down in a household of virtual strangers . . . too young for any kind of resignation, too old for transplant without shock. Was that what gave her her shell, her look of aloofness, the air of challenge she wore as nonchalantly as a glove?

Sentry got up abruptly, not wanting to remember too clearly the single isolated moment when Sarah's shell had cracked disastrously wide, when the blaze of anger between them had burnt away everything but the touch of her shoulders and the knowledge of her mouth. Had Sarah felt anything at all during that one instant in his arms? Hardly, thought Sentry, allowing himself a pause for clinical recollection; Sarah was good at that kind of thing, and had the advantage of practice.

The cottage shuddered under a new burst of the storm, and a bough of the apple tree hit the roof with a jolting crack. Sentry went to bed wondering if he would find himself in the cove by morning.

But by morning the storm had lost its fury and dwindled to a spiritless rain, oddly quiet after the tumult of the day before. At about four o'clock the sun came out on flattened gardens, toppling fences, broken trees, a harbor still ruffled by the remembrance of wind. Armed with directions, Sentry drove out along the road that led to Sutter's Point.

He found the little stone bridge where Eleanora Ware had died. A rocky cove lay below it on one side, on the other rose a wooded hillside. It was very quiet now; there was only the small curling sound of waves on the shore and an occasional leafy stir in the trees above. Far out on the smoked-silver water Sentry could see the tip of Sutter's Point and the outlines of a ruined house, the only building on the barren finger of land and rock.

Sands must have felt quite safe.

Sentry got back into his car and drove another two miles

along the narrow twisting badly-patched road without seeing a driveway or a mailbox. He found the explanation for that in a housing development that swarmed unexpectedly up out of the tangled green countryside; a wide highway led out of it into the town, making the other half of a circle. The old road had obviously been in disuse for years.

Sentry went back to the little bridge and parked his car just beyond it. He had noticed before a sandy cut leading up the hillside about twenty yards from the spot where Eleanora Ware's car had crashed. Mightn't Sands have panicked in those first few seconds after the impact; mightn't he have headed blindly off the road before chance headlights could find him?

He must have done something like that. Because that was where Sentry's reconstruction fell down badly, almost to the cancellation point. If Nick had witnessed the actual crash, Eleanora Ware might not have died, would certainly not have died where she lay. Therefore Nick hadn't seen it. But—heard it? And, a stranger to the town, further disoriented by darkness and rain, not been able to locate the direction of the sound?

Sentry got his answer moments later when he pushed away a cedar branch and stood at the top of the hill. Before him was a summerhouse flanked by wine-glass elms; the grayed and tilted gravestones of an old cemetery covered a slope that led down to a pond. He had seen that pond before, an old man had told him proudly, "Ain't no bottom to it."

At a distance from the gradual flattening of the hill, partially obscured by trees but plainly recognizable from the fountaining shape of the maples in its yard, was the Trellishaw house.

So that was that. A short-cut, Jane Trellishaw had said, over the hill and across the fields. It patched up the one gaping hole in his theory, it gave him at the same time a feeling that should have been exultation but was instead a cold ebbing sensation in his stomach.

From the direction of the bridge and the cut in the hillside, it must have been approximately here that Nick had heard the sound of metal smashing against stone. He had to have been here in order to acquire his dangerous knowledge, if, as Sentry assumed, Sands had run wildly up the hill to avoid a chance encounter on the road. And Nick had——

Sentry stopped dead, remembering for the first time the question that had been forming in his mind outside the doctor's office when he had been interrupted by the sound of a car horn.

On a night further blackened and blotted by rain, how had Nick recognized Sands?

As an intimate of the Trellishaws' Sands would need no guidance in this part of the town; wouldn't, in any case, have dared to show a light in his headlong flight. Nick himself used a cigarette lighter, had ever since a serious burn from an exploding matchbook——

A cigarette lighter.

It came together for Sentry then. He had had this particular answer all along; Jane Trellishaw had given it to him, casually, cloaking something else. ". . . As a matter of fact, Nick lost a cigarette lighter en route. One of the Thatcher boys—they live up on the other side of the pond—brought it back a few weeks later."

How might Sands have reacted to a sudden revealing brilliance in the dark? With an instinctive violence, a swift hand striking at the lighter, not in time to prevent one deadly instant of recognition? It was believable, even logical; it was still only a shadow key for a shadow lock. Sentry ground a heel savagely into the wet earth—and suddenly it was more than that.

He noticed for the first time that he was standing at the edge of a narrow worn path that led across the hilltop. Below him, twelve feet away, the path disappeared among pines; on the upper slant it stopped at a crumbling stone wall and continued on the other side. Sentry followed it to the wall and gazed up at the roof and chimney of a house almost hidden by intervening trees. The Thatcher house, undoubtedly. Which meant that the path leading up to it had been instituted, or at least deepened, by the Thatcher boys—which in turn indicated that when one of them had found the lighter it had lain on the path or near it. Directly in line with the point at which Sands would have emerged in his racing climb from the road to the hilltop.

Coincidence—that Nick had lost a lighter at all on the night of Eleanora Ware's death, that he had lost it at this vantage point on the hill? Hardly. It was the statement, cold, clear, shocking, of why Nick had had to die. Nick had stood not far from where Sentry stood now, startled perhaps by the sound of running feet; he had flicked on his lighter and a recognized face had leaped at him out of rainy darkness. He had known the face when he saw it again at Cabanatuan, and he had known by then the fact and the manner of Eleanora Ware's death and the significance of that fragmentary meeting . . .

A sudden rustling of branches, a small crackling progress of leaves and twigs brought Sentry's head up sharply. He had crushed out his cigarette and was halfway down the hill before it occurred to him that there had been, in that hot sunny silence, no breath of wind at all.

12

IT TOOK SENTRY a moment to react to the knock at the front door at nine o'clock that evening. There was first of all the rapid and instinctive feeling that this was not his house, that it might be a total stranger waiting on the porch, and there was, disturbingly, the image of Sarah, whom he had seen late that afternoon when he drove slowly back through the town.

A different and somehow astonishing Sarah, wearing something crisp and white on top and something billowy and plaid below, carrying a grocery bag so packed that there were celery tops tickling her chin. She had seen his car halted at the curb; she was probably, Sentry had thought, the only woman east of the Mississippi who could look detached with such a burden. To his bland offer of a lift she said politely, "Oh no, thanks, Andrew. But we'll be seeing you tomorrow, won't we? I believe you made quite an impression," this was unmistakably grim, "on my Aunt Jane."

"Your Aunt Jane," Sentry had said, offensively benign, "is a very charming creature."

She had been about to answer that when a horn sounded lightly and an ash-blue DeSoto convertible pulled abreast of Sentry's car. Charles Farrar was at the wheel; Megan, the sun turning her childishly straight hair to flax, was beside him. Greetings were exchanged; Sentry drove away with the feeling that, given a moment more, Sarah might have said something that mattered.

But she wouldn't come here to the cottage to say it—or would she? Sentry crossed the tiny living room and opened the front door and said in astonishment, "Cy! I thought you were safely tucked away at Tim's—how come? You're in luck, though, we still have one room available."

Cy was rosy and delighted, stooping expertly through the doorway in his enormous shabby tweeds. "I can't stay. My God, this place is small—you forget. I'm spending the week-end with Aunt Augusta, she's got a tenant coming after Labor Day. Tell you what, I'll have a drink, at gunpoint."

Sentry got out a bottle and said he thought the expression "rum weather" must mean just that. After drinks had been poured Cy volunteered that he had taken the train and then the bus from Boston, arriving about an hour ago. "How are you? Everything all right here?" There was, once more, that transition to blundering solicitude. "Been getting a rest?"

Sentry said casually that he had. He let a long comfortable interval go by before he remarked, "I didn't know you knew the Trellishaws."

Cy's glass stopped halfway to his lips. He said in amazement, "Good Lord, do you know them?"

It was the last response Sentry had expected; it threw him into momentary confusion. Cy said, "I told you I'd met your brother once. I guess I forgot about its being up here. My Aunt Augusta's a great pal of Jane Trellishaw's—they were very nice to me the summer she was abroad. As a matter of fact I haven't seen the Trellishaws for years."

"But you know Sarah Devany, of course."

"I met Sarah a couple of times up here that summer, I've run into her once or twice in New York. And if you'd like to know why I didn't mention that in the beginning," said Cy a little stiffly, "it was because at the time I met you, if you'll recall, chit-chat about Sarah Devany and her relatives was strictly not the order of the day. You felt strongly on the subject, like Lizzie Borden."

He had taken off his glasses and was polishing them with unusual devotion and energy for Cy; Sentry, watching him, saw his perplexity and hurt and was suddenly ashamed of himself. He said, "You mean those days when I was a two-bottle man?" and Cy grinned. "You've gone to the other extreme. Can't you pry the cork out of that jug? And then I've got to get back."

The tension evaporated, but it had been there in a cloaked accusation, an edge of anger. Sentry was insistent that Cy stay at the cottage, he would take the upstairs room. Cy shook his head. "I wouldn't stay here in any case. I see Aunt Augusta so seldom that she makes a point of it, and besides that she's getting ready for this tenant. You know—floors to be sanded, shutters painted, things like that. If I were over here I'd sleep till noon, and well she knows it."

He was at the door, had it open on darkness, when he stopped and said slowly, "There's one other thing. It's mainly why I haven't seen the Trellishaws for so long, or talked about them. There was a girl, the older of Mrs. Trellishaw's daughters by a former marriage. Her name was Eleanora. I—she and I . . ."

Cy broke off, fumbling noisily in one bulging pocket for cigarettes. Sentry got out his own and extended them, glad not to look at the sudden somberness that big anxious friendly Cy wore so awkwardly. Cy took a cigarette and said, "Thanks. The thing is that she was killed in a car crash the summer I met her. She was only twenty-four, and she was . . . well, hell."

When he lifted his head from the match flame he was back to a reassuring normal. He said wryly, "Throw this man out, he's breaking my heart. I'll probably see you around tomorrow. So long . . ."

Sentry made himself a nightcap and sat up late with it, putting things together in his mind. Cy Stevenson and Eleanora Ware . . . combined, they made an odd interlocking piece that didn't fit with anything else. Not with what he knew of Cy, not with what he had heard about Eleanora.

Nor with anything else, because no man would leave a girl he loved to die alone in the dark.

Except . . . Sands, who had already shown himself as violently different from other men, who wiped out by his very continuing existence all the blind and comfortable standards of civilized behavior. Sands, who was fastidious, who had killed three people without ever lifting a weapon.

Before he went to bed Sentry opened the bureau drawer that held the Colt .45, lifted the gun out, put a clip in it and slid it gently back. It crossed his mind with a faint feeling of surprise that the shining bluish thing in among his handkerchiefs did not look melodramatic at all.

Saturday was so clear and still and hot that it might have been weather under glass; sky and water and light-drenched rocks had an edged, scalding brilliance. At around noon Sentry picked his way cautiously down the cliff at the back of the cottage and went for a swim in the cove. The water looked lucid and inviting; the impact of it drove the breath out of his lungs. He swam out a few yards and swam rapidly back, his forehead and wrists aching with cold. The huge tilting rocks at the foot of the cliff were warm in the sun. He smoked a cigarette, stretched out in a skin of fire and ice, and climbed back up to the cottage.

It was Jane Trellishaw, her brown aquiline face friendly, who came around the corner of the white-shuttered yellow house to greet him. "It's so nice to see you, Mr. Sentry, but I wish you'd brought a breeze. Isn't it hot? I'm beginning to lose my faith in storms, they never seem to break up anything but the trees you're fondest of."

She waved a rueful hand at a maple branch lying on the lawn. "You see? And it's so hot again that nobody has the energy to do anything about it. But come on around back, we're all outside. I hope you don't mind open-air food . . . ?"

Sentry told her he was a great open-air man and also, as it happened, a great food man. They rounded the corner of the house into a sudden tree-enclosed Town and Country area of lawn and deck chairs and a group of people who instantly shifted and broke at the new arrival. Sentry had just time to think with quiet satisfaction, Old Home Week. Good, couldn't be better, when the men were lazily on their feet and a thin dark woman whom he had never seen before was coming toward him.

Jane said, "Harriet, this is Andrew Sentry—Nick's brother. Mr. Sentry, my sister-in-law, Mrs. Howard Trellishaw."

Megan Ware's mother was in her fifties, with huge beautiful dark eyes in a haggard battered face that had had only the cursory attention of a lipstick. Someone had evidently told her once that she had speaking eyes; she inclined her head silently and gave Sentry a rich upward glance as she took his hand. The glance was obviously intended to say that she was delighted to meet him and pleased that he had been able to come; Mrs. Trellishaw herself, disconcertingly, said nothing at all. As she turned away Sentry had a swift glimpse of a profiled nose and chin that had once, probably, been delicate and intriguing, but were now on their way to a point of rendezvous. In ten years Harriet Trellishaw would be witchlike; even at the moment, for Sentry she had a faintly sinister air.

Cy Stevenson said heartily, "Beat you to it, Andrew. But I have priority, these are old friends of mine." James Court said,

◈ 125

smiling, "Nice to see you. Seems a long way from New York, doesn't it, thank God?" Charles Farrar, scrubbed and impeccable in a cord coat and flannels, was anxious and a little stiff. "Glad to see you, Sentry. Pretty place, isn't it? Let me get you a drink . . ."

From a deck chair Megan Ware smiled and nodded at Sentry; he watched her eyes go instantly to her mother. And then Sarah was there, saying composedly, "Hello, Andrew. You've been swimming."

"Through a hole in the ice, yes." He gave her a mild glance of inquiry.

"Your hair's wet." Sarah glanced quickly away and then back at him, her gray eyes direct. A random dapple of sunlight flickered across her face. "Did you have to come here, Andrew? I work fairly hard all year, I thought I'd earned a vacation."

"Don't we all?" said Sentry pleasantly.

"I won't be watched," Sarah said, suddenly furious, "and, damn you, Andrew, I won't have my apartment——"

"Whisky sour," said Charles Farrar affably at Sentry's elbow. "How about you, Sarah, ready for another?"

"No, I'm not," Sarah said edgily. "But I don't think Andrew's seen the duck pond. Why don't you show him, Charles? Be awfully careful that he doesn't fall in."

"Right," said Charles cheerfully, and began to lead the way.

Sentry followed him docilely. He thought, James Court—natural enough, he's interested in Sarah, he timed his vacation to fit hers. Farrar's the future son-in-law here, and a nice layout it is—nothing odd about that. Cy has a fairly special acquaintance with these people; it would look funny if he didn't drop in sooner or later.

Unless he was wrong all the way, one of these men was, had to be Sands.

They had come to a stop beyond the ragged fringe of apple trees. Sentry turned his head and stared sharply at Charles Farrar, trying to see behind the waxy, well-shaven, rather forceless face. Farrar wasn't looking at him, he was gesturing at a pond with three snowy ducks poised stiffly at the far edge.

"There they are. A brook runs through there and gives them a change of water."

Sentry gazed at them, trying to think of something penetrating to offer about ducks. They looked like cunning decoys, white, motionless, too lifelike to be real. He needn't have bothered. Farrar said, watching the water, "I couldn't help overhearing when Sarah started to tell you about her apartment being broken into. Frankly, Mr. Sentry, I didn't like the sound of that at all. A woman alone in New York"—there was an unmistakable sound here of trailing draperies and smelling salts— "takes something of a risk anyway. But an actual breaking and entering——!"

"When was this?"

"Monday night—the night I put Megan on the train and, I think, Sarah dined with you and Court. I gather from Megan that Sarah put in a panicky call to Jane, and Sarah, as you know, isn't the kind of girl who panics. It doesn't matter when it happened, it's that it happened at all."

"I see what you mean," murmured Sentry. He lighted a cigarette and threw the match into the pond. So this was to be the explanation of the non-appearance of Nick's letters—Sarah had mislaid them in her apartment after all and then a burglar had taken them. It was so childish that it was laughable, and yet, he knew it very well, incontrovertible. But he could still let her see that he didn't believe it, he could still——

Farrar was talking haltingly, a little shyly. "When you and Sarah get back from vacation, you'll both be in New York.

Megan and I—you've probably heard—are going to be married in September, and we'll be living in Philadelphia. You're—interested in Sarah. She's Megan's cousin, after all, and we owe her a lot. If you could keep an eye out, maybe go to the police discreetly if there's any further disturbance . . ."

Discretion, thought Sentry, was Farrar's touchstone. He listened to a flapping of white wings and said dryly, "I think the ducks have had enough of us. Yes, as a matter of fact, I'm very interested in Sarah . . ."

He didn't have a chance to corner her immediately. There was lunch, with charcoal-broiled steaks and salad and garlic bread and cold beer. When Jane Trellishaw went into the house for replenishments Sentry followed her. In the kitchen, while she opened more bottles and put empties back in a case, he learned two illuminating things.

One, that Howard Trellishaw had been a sleeping partner in Consolidated Chemicals, the gilt-edged corporation that introduced more new drugs, retained bigger research laboratories and took glossier advertising space than any of its competitors. It had, Sentry knew, swallowed up a dozen small independent companies in half as many years. Its subsidiaries were everywhere, in paints, fabrics, cosmetics. Whoever married one of the Ware girls would have come in, if he were patient, for a considerable sum of money.

Two, that Howard Trellishaw had unofficially taken James Court, the son of an old friend, into the place of the son he could never have. Had groomed him for a key position at Consolidated Chemicals, had contemplated with pleasure an eventual marriage between Court and his step-daughter, Eleanora Ware.

Jane was quiet and thoughtful, leaning against the kitchen table. "Sarah's probably told you about Eleanora."

"It must have been a terrible shock to you all," Sentry said sincerely, and blessed Sarah's reticence once more.

Jane nodded. "It was, of course—but in a way it was worst of all for my brother. Eleanora had always been his favorite; that was why he never said anything at all about her to James. It was the old prove-yourself-first theory, I suppose, and there are worse ones. But of course he couldn't help wondering, afterwards, if he wasn't partly to blame. If there had been a marriage, or even an engagement . . ."

What if there had been, in secret? At any rate, what Jane Trellishaw had told him opened up an entirely new avenue. Sentry dismissed it abruptly when he found an opportunity to corner Sarah under an apple tree at the side of the house.

"McIntoshes," said Sarah brightly, turning her back to scoop up an apple. "They're wonderful, really. Of course, we haven't had the trees sprayed properly . . ."

"Sarah," said Sentry briskly.

She turned mutely to face him.

"If I'm not mistaken," Sentry said pleasantly, "this is where Nick's letters are—up at your aunt's in the country. You can get hold of them now, can't you, Sarah? I'm very anxious to see them. I'll wait here, shall I?"

He transferred his gaze to the ground quickly; he was through, he told himself firmly, with that lost white look. He was startled at the cool sound of Sarah's voice.

"You'd better not wait, Andrew, because it may take a while. I asked Jane as soon as I got here, and she said she'd put the letters in the vault. Luckily the bank manager's a friend of hers, and though the bank's closing just about now I ought to be able to get them if I leave right away."

"Good," said Sentry, cloaking his surprise. "Will I come here, or what?"

Sarah hesitated. Then she said, "I don't see any reason for embroiling everybody else in this. I know where Cy's cottage is. Suppose I bring the letters to you after dinner—about nine?"

"Nine it is," said Sentry.

He wondered, as he thanked Harriet Trellishaw and received a throaty and mysterious goodbye, as he shook Jane Trellishaw's hard brown hand, what Sarah meant to do about this latest development. She had withheld the letters before, under cover of a palpable lie, presumably to protect someone. Had she decided now that there was no need for protection?

Sentry had dinner in the cottage out of a can that said stew. By the time he had made coffee it was twenty minutes of nine; he mocked at himself for setting out an extra cup, emptying the ashtrays, straightening the tumbled bookcase—Sarah Devany, if she came, would be there for a single businesslike instant. She wouldn't notice if the armchair's cushion sagged, the hearth was feathered with ashes. When he had finished his housewifely rounds he had only five minutes to wait—and all at once not even that. A car must have driven up while he was splashing water at the sink; at any rate there was the sliding gravelly sound of footsteps in the driveway.

Sarah was early; so much the better. Nevertheless, as he crossed the room, threw the porch light switch and opened the door, Sentry found himself distrusting this sudden eagerness on her part. Unless—but would she dare?—she had come without Nick's letters, and was anxious to get over what she knew would be a short and unpleasant scene.

As indeed it would be. Sentry, standing in the open doorway and looking out on darkness beyond the dim spread of the living room lights, realized that the footsteps had stopped, realized why. The porch light switch hadn't caught when he flipped it.

He called sharply, "Hold it, I'll get a light," and stretched back a reaching arm. The switch clicked again, uselessly.

"I'll come down and give you a hand," Sentry said resignedly into the darkness, and crossed the porch and went gingerly down the wooden steps at the side. "Where are you, Sarah? There's a little slope to your right and then the steps——"

As he said it, before the words were through, he felt a sudden cold wariness. But even then he was totally unprepared for the hurtling rush that came at him out of the dark. Something struck agonizingly over his right eye; he remembered thinking, That was a rock. He lifted his shoulders jarringly from the edge of the steps and tried to make a frantic half-turn under the weight that pinned him there. Then the darkness was seeping under his eyelids, had flooded into his brain.

13

Sᴀɴᴅs ʜᴀᴅ sᴛᴀʀᴛᴇᴅ to kill him.

Physical contact had told him that his attacker was a man. His brain, and the rooted intimacy of his hatred, knew that the man was Sands.

In the abstract it was logical, even to be expected. In actuality it was queerly appalling to have grappled in the dark with someone who had intended to end your life, to have touched with your own hands the shape of the man who up until that moment had been only a murderous image.

Sentry lay motionless in the bed. There was a light blanket over him, he could feel the softness of it under his fingers. He thought that he was probably in the bedroom in Cy Stevenson's cottage, and he was aware that there was someone near him. He didn't care who. He was, for the moment, wrapped up in his throbbing blinding forehead—all of him was wrapped up in it, every pulse, every nerve gathered together in a wet tangle of pain.

Fabric stirred on itself, something creaked. Light tiptoeing footsteps receded and then came back, up to the edge of the bed. Sarah, thought Sentry, knowing it, and all at once a misty wave of anger came welling up in him. That was bad; it started the blood hammering woundingly in his head. He kept his eyelids stubbornly closed. After seconds of silence the chair creaked again and there was the sound of a match striking.

When he thought she was safely established with her cigarette Sentry opened his eyes cautiously. The light, dim as it was, seemed swordlike. He tried it again, more slowly, and saw the familiar chintz curtains, the bureau, the doorway into the living room. And Sarah Devany in the only armchair, her face white and distracted, regarding him fixedly.

She said shakily, "Well . . . !" and crossed to the bed. "Does it feel awful, Andrew? Don't move your head."

"I'm flattered," said Sentry, finding his tongue thick and unwilling, "that you think I can."

"The doctor ought to be here any minute. Meanwhile," said Sarah, watching him nervously, "I don't think you should even be talking."

"Not by rights," Sentry said. Speech was an effort; it was as though every word were being tapped out in Braille against his temples. "But it didn't quite come off, did it, Sarah?"

She stared at him for a long instant. Then she said curtly, "You're out of your head. You'd better not try to talk at all, really," and went to stand at one of the dark windows.

There were a great many things that Sentry would have liked to shout at her straight challenging back. That only he and Sarah had known of their nine o'clock appointment—and that he had told no one. That he had been suspicious, even that afternoon, of her willingness to deliver the letters. That——

The letters. Nick's. They were all at once floaty and elusive; Sentry tried to pin them down and moved his head impatiently and broke out slowly in a drenching perspiration. At a great distance Sarah whispered, "That's the doctor . . ."

He didn't see her go. He was aware of James Court suddenly in the doorway, looking wider awake than usual, and of Dr. H. Addison Palmer shouldering past him, eight feet tall in tan gabardine. Palmer paused at the bedside and gave Sentry a long protuberant black stare. "Well, well, Mr. Sentry, we meet again." The eyelids dropped, the teeth, all sixty-four of them, flashed in snowy amusement. "What's the trouble—been in a fight?"

Sentry didn't see the rapid competent fingers laying things out on the bed, couldn't measure the quick diagnosis in the lazy eyes. He was aware only of his own engulfing rage—at himself, at Sands, at Sarah for betraying him, at the thunderous throbbing of his head. He said distinctly, "Not at all. I happened to be walking down the steps on my head, that's all, and I slipped."

"Right," said Palmer, grinning and unruffled. He turned his head fractionally to say over his shoulder, "How long's it been? Forty minutes? . . . I'd like a basin of warm water and a couple of towels; we'll have to see what's under this mess."

It was over an hour before he packed the black bag again. He washed and probed and took eleven stitches, dressed and bandaged the wound on Sentry's head, noted down pulse and temperature and blood pressure. He said, towelling his hands, "I'll want a prescription filled."

James Court stepped out of the shadows beyond the lamp. "I'll take care of that, Doctor."

"Right. Now, there's got to be someone with him tonight. I'll be around first thing in the morning to see what the concussion's doing. Where's the phone?"

Sentry, weak and light-headed, lay idly in his bed and listened. To Sarah: "There is none, Doctor. I can stay here until——"

Palmer: "It's—let's see—ten after eleven. I don't know who I'll be able to dig up at this hour but I'll give it a try. The thing is, someone's got to see that he takes this stuff every three hours, doesn't get chilled, doesn't move around."

"I can stay if you can't get a nurse," Sarah said. She sounded stifled. Sentry took it all in with mild and amiable interest; he had had a hypodermic and these people seemed unduly confused and anxious, but very pleasant. Palmer and Court left, still in conversation, and a moment later Court was back and Sarah was administering two coral-colored pills. Sentry went to sleep while they were arguing pointlessly over some car or other.

He woke in darkness. His mouth was dry and his head hurt, but it was a healthy healing pain. He put out an automatic hand to the night table for his cigarettes, and the darkness moved instantly. Sarah said softly, "What is it, Andrew?"

Sarah . . . the foggy patches cleared. They hadn't been able to arrange for a nurse. Sentry said he would like a cigarette, and she hesitated and then said, "I don't see why not. I'll stay here, though, just in case you get sleepy." He took the cigarette from her fingers in the dark, narrowed his eyes against the sudden match flame. Sarah said, lighting her own, "It's nearly time for your pills. How do you feel?"

"As though I'd been hit over the head with a rock. Otherwise, fine. This can't be very pleasant for you, by the way."

"I don't mind."

There was a pause. Sarah's cigarette tip swung up in an arc, brightened, and went down again. "Andrew—as long as you're awake and chatty, do you remember anything at all of what happened to you?"

Sentry caught himself on the brink of saying sharply, "Everything." He couldn't have put his finger on the wariness that stopped him, that brought out the doubtful, "Not very clearly. I know that the porch was dark, and that I thought I heard you coming up the driveway and went out and cracked my head on something. Does that jibe with anything?"

Sarah took in a small gentle breath; Sentry could have sworn it was relief. She told him that she had driven up to the cottage at about nine, maybe two minutes of, and had seen that the front door was open. When she had gotten no answer to her call she had returned to her car, parked at the side of the road, for her flashlight. It was on her way back up to the cottage that she had found Sentry at the foot of the tilting rock slabs to one side of the wooden steps.

At the foot of the rocks . . . five feet away and up to the right of where he had been pinned against a cutting wooden edge. He had been dragged there, of course, because it was conceivable that a man might walk off the edge of the porch in darkness and, in falling, strike his head against the lifting lips of rock.

And Sands always killed without weapons.

Sarah was saying in a rush, "I knew I couldn't get you into the house by myself. I drove back to the house and by sheer luck caught James—James Court—just leaving. He came over with me and we carried you in and—that's all. I'll get your pills."

Sentry tried to tackle the implications of what she had told him, but the pleasant, dully throbbing languor caught him again. And then Sarah was back, saying, "I'm afraid I'll have to turn on a light for this," and supporting his head with her arm while she handed him the pills and a glass of water.

"It's after two o'clock. Go back to sleep," she said, and unexpectedly stooped and smoothed the light blanket across his chest, tucking it under at the side. Sentry said half-mockingly, "Aren't you going to kiss your little boy goodnight?"

Sarah stared for an instant. They had talked companionably enough in the dark; it was as if the light, the knowledge of each other's eyes, brought out the old challenges. She looked very tall standing there beside the bed, the lamplight behind her fringing her hair raggedly with gold. She said calmly, "If you like," and bent. The brush of her lips was chastely for his cheek;

◈ *136*

Sentry, turning his head at the last fractional second, caught a corner of her mouth.

Sarah straightened as though she had been burned. Sentry was instantly angry, at himself for an unbidden impulse, at Sarah for anticipating it. He said, exaggerating his drowsiness, "As I think you remarked before, I'm out of my head . . . these damned pills."

"They're quite strong," Sarah said expressionlessly. "See you at five, Andrew."

Five in the morning was an eerie time, half night-hush, half day-sounds. A wash of gray in the sky, darkness lingering in the apple boughs, a freshening lift of air that brought along the cheeping of birds who had apparently been up and about for hours. Sentry came awake to Sarah's voice saying, "Andrew? . . . Andrew, your pills."

"In a minute," Sentry murmured, recomposing himself instantly for sleep.

"Now," said Sarah inexorably. "Please, Andrew, and then you can go off again for as long as you like."

But he couldn't. His head was better, so much better that he wondered a little at all the care and anxiety. It ached, of course, a steady dull undertone that jarred into pain when he moved it, and the stitches felt like the lacing of a football. In spite of that and the slightly drunken feeling that came from a night of sleeping pills, there were things he wanted to know too badly to bury himself in sleep again. Sarah said at last, "I've made coffee. I don't suppose it would hurt—would you like a cup?"

She brought him toast with it. Sentry, who had felt his way cautiously into a propped-up position, lighted a cigarette and felt oddly guilty as he said, "By the way, Sarah, you have the letters, haven't you?"

◆ 137

Sarah glanced away. She had brushed her hair and washed her face and put on fresh clear lipstick; she looked more like the brisk cool New York Sarah than the pale preoccupied girl who had guarded him during the night. But the gathering of her forces was still apparent.

"That's what I came to tell you last night—that the letters are gone, Andrew. It seems that Jane intended to put them in the vault and then didn't, although she thought she had. Anyway, they're—not there. I'm sorry . . ."

Whatever had happened to the letters, thought Sentry, watching her closely, that wasn't it. She had lied in the first place, he was sure of it, in saying they were up here at her aunt's house at all. She had had an odd driven air when he accosted her about the letters yesterday afternoon. She had seemed very calm and direct immediately afterwards, but there had been that single moment when she braced herself for something. And lastly, Jane Trellishaw hadn't impressed Sentry as the kind of woman who got confused as to where she had put things—things, particularly, that would be accorded a certain kind of value.

Sentry let it drop for the moment, knowing from Sarah's rigid poise that he would get no more out of her at the moment. He asked instead about the breaking into and search of her apartment, and received a wide and faintly accusing stare.

"But didn't you—wasn't that your doing, Andrew?"

Sentry assured her that it had not been. "If it had I'd have taken the etching over the desk, which I presume was still there?"

Sarah nodded without smiling; she had a hunted look. She said abruptly, "You'd better get what sleep you can before the doctor comes," and left the room with an unmistakable air of escape.

◈ *138*

So that was that, temporarily. Had he actually hoped she would bring him the letters, the postcard that—he was almost certain of it now—would pass on Nick's recognition of Sands? In the middle of savage contemplation, Sentry dropped into a half-waking dream.

At nearly eight, in a tide of burning sunlight across the bed, he woke again. Sarah brought him more coffee and a glass of tomato juice; he saw by full daylight that there were ashy shadows under her clear eyes. He said, "Have you got a car, Sarah?" and saw her nod. "Then why don't you go home? You've been roaming around all night while I slept like a stone. I wish you hadn't been let in for this—you look like the devil."

Sarah said, "I'm all right," and turned quickly away from him to do something unnecessary at the bureau-top, as though she didn't like his measuring gaze on her tired face.

Afterwards, Sentry tried to trace it back, the sudden sharpness that went plunging through his mind. He knew later that it was partly Sarah's action and partly his own anger and contempt at himself for having walked out into the unanswering dark like a trusting child—he, who had lived for over a week with the murderous shadow of Sands, who had a loaded gun in his bureau drawer and had gone down the steps defenseless, unwary until it was too late.

Palmer would be here soon. Sentry said quickly, "Do me a favor, before you go. There's a gun in that top right-hand drawer, under the handkerchiefs. Get it for me, will you? It's loaded, so be careful."

Sarah gave him a quick white look and went to the bureau. She pulled out the drawer and put a hand inside; Sentry knew a long waiting moment before she said, "Could you have put it somewhere else, Andrew? There isn't anything here but handkerchiefs."

◈ *139*

14

SENTRY SPENT SUNDAY confined to his bed.

"Day of rest," Palmer informed him cheerfully that morning. "I'll want X rays later to be on the safe side, but as far as I can tell there's no fracture. I'd cut out the sedative for today, take it tonight before you go to sleep." He glanced at his watch. "There's a Miss Tibbett, a practical nurse, on her way here. She'll get your meals and change the dressing and see that you don't go out dancing."

He picked up his hat and bag. Sentry said that he didn't need a nurse, that he could take it easy by himself.

"Oh, you can?" Palmer said ironically. "Concussion's tricky. There's no phone here. Suppose you get dizzy—it happens—and have another spell. Suppose—" he gave Sentry a straight unsmiling glance "—you take a notion to walk down the steps on your head again. You mightn't be so lucky the next time, Mr. Sentry. I'll drop by tonight and see what's what."

Sentry stopped him. "As you go out, would you mind seeing if the porch light works?"

The switch flicked an instant later. Palmer came back to the bedroom doorway and said expressionlessly, "It doesn't because there's no bulb in it. That the cause of the accident?"

"Contributing," Sentry said grimly.

Palmer nodded. He withdrew his head, said, "Watch it. I'll see you," and was gone.

Well, thought Sentry, digesting the tone of that, Palmer would know, of course, from a thorough examination of the wound in his head. But doctors were used to not asking questions, and if Palmer had found traces of two or more blows in the same spot over his temple, he would still accept the story he had been given unless he were asked officially for an opinion.

Which he would not be; Sentry had made up his mind to that. Let it pass for the moment as a clumsy trip in the dark. Sands would know that Sentry knew otherwise; it made a direct and dangerous bond between them. And Sands couldn't be sure that Sentry hadn't confided in someone; Sands, who had never muffed a killing before, might grow nervous. He had the elements of panic in him to begin with—that was what had made him leave Eleanora Ware dying in a smashed-up car.

Let the panic grow. Feed it a little . . .

Meanwhile, a few unarguable facts had emerged. He had switched on the porch light on the evening Cy Stevenson had dropped in, the evening before the attack on him; he had taken the Colt out of his bureau drawer and loaded it that same night. The following day, Saturday, he had gone for a swim in the cove, and the cottage had been empty for roughly twenty-five minutes. After lunch at the Trellishaws' he had come back here, and had driven into town later for cigarettes and food.

Had he announced his intention of that at the Trellishaws'? It was more than possible; someone had been asking him politely what he did about meals. It must have been that, Sentry thought suddenly; it had to be.

Because Sands had known he would be alone and waiting at nine o'clock last night. Sands had made his preparations accordingly—the removal of the porch-light bulb, the theft of the Colt—necessarily after he learned of the appointment with Sarah Devany, made under the apple tree at the side of the house. There had been no one in a position to overhear, the others had trailed inside. Sarah would have followed them if Sentry hadn't stopped her.

Sarah had informed a third person of their arrangements for that evening. It shouldn't have been hard to realize—she had lied to him about the letters from the beginning—but somehow the added knowledge still carried a fresh shock for Sentry. He had felt it for the first time in her small breath of relief when he had said he remembered nothing of his accident. Was it compunction, then, that had made Sarah volunteer for her long and sleepless night of attendance?

Forget it, Sentry thought. Sarah mattered only as a valuable link to the Trellishaws, and because of her nearness to Sands. If he could be patient, if he could keep his own cold knowledge cloaked and unsuspected, Sarah would lead him to Sands . . .

Miss Tibbett, the nurse, was elderly, capable, and gloomy. She made it clear within ten minutes of her arrival that she was too old to be out drudging like this and only did it for the sake of her sick widowed sister, and that the bottle of rum which she subsequently found in the kitchen was at the bottom of the whole sordid accident. She caught Sentry at about ten o'clock in a barefoot and desperate search for cigarettes, and shook her head blightingly.

"You'll never get better at this rate, I can tell you that, Mr. Sentry. A man in your condition! And not getting any younger, either."

"No," said Sentry; it wasn't a point that admitted of much argument. He got back into bed and found that it was a refuge, that his few wandering steps had brought on a thin clinging dampness and a jogging pain in his head. Miss Tibbett, still grim, followed him and with a few Houdini-like gestures drew the sheets taut and smooth under and over him.

Sentry closed his eyes and thought soberly that in future it might be wise to save all his cigarette stubs. After all, you never knew. He was at the edge of a thwarted half-doze when there was a commotion at the front door and Cy Stevenson arrived.

Cy put an anxious face around the bedroom doorway with exaggerated caution. Light from the window struck across his glasses. "Well, isn't this a hell of a thing?" He came on into the room, concerned behind a surface grin, to stand at the foot of the bed. "Sure you weren't going to sleep or something? How's the head?"

"No worse than sleeping under a bowling alley. How's your cigarette supply?"

Cy, who had started to shake his own head commiseratingly, put a package on the table beside the bed. "I've got more in the car—which reminds me, I'd have been here before this if Aunt Augusta hadn't been out in it all morning showing a house. I thought you or" he nodded at the inner regions of the cottage, "might want some errands run. Gosh, I got a jolt when Sarah phoned me. I suppose you've got your lawyers all lined up?"

Something froze inside Sentry; a second later he said cheerfully, "Sure. I'm going to take you for everything you've got, except your suits. Only trouble is to make it look like somebody's fault but mine, which may hold me up a bit."

Cy sat forward in the armchair. "What'd you do, anyway, start out for a walk and miss your footing? The porch is so damn narrow I can see that part of it. But the bulb," said Cy, looking worried, "should have been in the porch lamp. Sarah said it was dark when she got here, so I checked just now. It was working Friday night when I came over, wasn't it? Bulbs don't walk away."

"Kids," Sentry said casually.

"Well . . ." Cy frowned over that. "There's practically none of that stuff in this town—the kids have the beach and the boat-yards. Lord, people don't even lock their doors most of the time."

And they get their guns stolen for their pains, Sentry thought grimly.

Cy glanced over his shoulder at the open doorway. He went up to the bed and said in a lowered voice, "Look, maybe I'm an old maid with the vapors over this—I hope so, anyway. But you know that business you had on your mind in New York before you came up here. When I first heard about your knock-ing your head on a rock I got half an idea you'd been—jumped. Anything in it?"

Miss Tibbett moved about distantly in the kitchen. Sentry turned his head fractionally so that he met Cy's eyes, steady, probing, in a waiting face that now held no easy good-humor at all. All right, he's worried, that's the kind of guy he is, Sen-try told himself angrily.

But he couldn't stop his own deliberately hesitant answer. "Not a thing, Cy. At least—no, it was one of those things where the ground takes a running jump at you. I'm ninety-nine per cent sure of it."

"Only ninety-nine?"

Sentry made himself grin. "You know how it is. I've seen too many movies, I guess—I keep having a feeling there's something I ought to remember."

Cy nodded. He said cheerfully, "Better not try too hard, your brains are sitting in a draught as it is. It'll come back. Any special missions before I go? I'll bet Miss What's-her-name has a few. See you . . ."

Listening to the exchange of voices in the kitchen, hearing Cy's departure, Sentry felt uncomfortable and vaguely ashamed of himself. He began an inner argument about that to the counterpoint of the swollen throbbing in his head.

Sands couldn't be quite sure, after all, that in Sentry's single moment of awareness before attack, there hadn't been something that could lead to recognition later. It couldn't have mattered much to Sands at the time because he was measuring Sentry's future in seconds. But something had happened to interrupt him—the sound of a car motor, the glow of headlights that meant Sarah's arrival—and it must matter very much to Sands now.

If Sentry mentioned his troubled half-recollection to enough of his visitors, sooner or later he would mention it to Sands.

Sands, who had the Colt, traceably Sentry's own. Sentry lay quiet and braced in the bed, looking at the possibilities of that, not liking any of them.

He had ample opportunity, that day and the next, to bring up his puzzling hint of memory. His visitors were frequent and sympathetic. Miss Tibbett said sourly, "This is a novel treatment for a head injury, I must say"; through Sentry's own mind ran a mocking quote carried over from childhood: 'King John said he was sorry, so did the Queen and Prince.'

Jane Trellishaw brought him cold chicken and jellied soup, she said apologetically, "I didn't know what you'd have on hand." From her, in a casual and roundabout way, Sentry learned that James Court had stayed at the Trellishaw house for dinner that Saturday evening, and after dinner had asked to go through some old files of Howard Trellishaw's. Jane was vague. "The company—Consolidated Chemicals—is having a fiftieth anniversary. They wanted some sort of statistics and an early customer letter or two, I think."

It sounded logical, it sounded true. But the files, Jane said,

◆ *145*

were in an unused bedroom upstairs—and it was also true that the stairs in that house were enclosed and led narrowly, quietly down to the front door in its smother of rambler roses. It wouldn't have taken Sands long to complete his errand. Not if he went up over the hill and through the old cemetery, and cut across the field opposite the cottage. Running, as Sands had run once before . . .

Sarah came and brought an armload of brightly-jacketed books. Megan Ware was with her, her huge dark eyes curious and—speculative? They didn't stay long. Sarah was studiedly casual, asking him what the doctor had said, if there was anything she could do while she was there. They were just on their way to the beach . . . Sentry thanked her and said no. He had a sudden unrelated wonder about Sarah at the beach. She wouldn't tan, with that hair, she would look very white in the cold lucid water. Strong shoulders, narrow waist, long legs— she ought to swim well.

What the hell is this? Sentry said to himself shockedly. When they left he had a peculiar sense of relief.

Charles Farrar came on Sunday evening with a bottle of superlative brandy which, at Sentry's insistence, he opened with an air of ritual. Miss Tibbett, humbled into silence by Farrar's aloof request, produced two small cheese glasses without demur.

"Well—literally—your health," Farrar said, smiling as he lifted his glass.

Sentry saluted him silently and tried to dismiss as ungrateful the impression of how at home Farrar looked in a sickroom. The consciously lowered voice, the scrubbed and gleaming cleanliness, the sober and solicitous attitude of concern—well, it's an Occasion, thought Sentry; small, but my own.

◈ *146*

The brandy glowed in his throat. Farrar leaned back in the small armchair and said mildly, "It's fortunate for Mr. Stevenson, isn't it, that you're such a good friend of his."

Sentry's eyebrows went up. Farrar said hastily, "Oh, I'm not serious. But legally, of course——"

"Legally I should be paying Cy rent."

"I understand that," said Farrar soothingly, "but it's a point, you know, that otherwise——" He glanced at Sentry and then away. "A head injury is still a head injury, even if you got it for nothing."

"It is indeed," Sentry said, wincing at a sudden throb. He waited until it died away again. "But it's no worse than—ever get thrown out of a jeep?"

Farrar shook his head, grimacing. "I've seen it happen. A sergeant in my company got pitched over a wall one day—he's still on a total disability pension. Another fellow——"

He stopped abruptly. Sentry saw the narrow strong fingers close in almost fracturing tension around the glass in Farrar's hand. He thought with what should have been triumph but was only an odd kind of pity, Something here . . . the root of the trouble, the cause of the crack-up?

He watched the blood come back to the whitened fingertips as Farrar set his glass carefully on the windowsill. The window was open on cool summer darkness, but a faint sheen was noticeable on Farrar's forehead. Sentry waited another moment and said casually, "Where was this?"

"Where—oh, New Guinea." Farrar spoke with an effort; he seemed like a man blinded and deafened and adrift in a private nightmare. His assurance, his smooth and comfortable conviction of his own dignity and worth had drained away from him; he was suddenly damp and unsure and frightened by the mere memory of fear.

Fear of something that had happened in New Guinea? Or in the Philippines? Four years out of your own life were, necessarily, four years out of everybody else's. If you were well away from your own town and the local newspapers, if there had been no correspondence, you could say you had been to Germany or Italy or Mars.

Or New Guinea.

Farrar had pulled himself together; Sentry realized later that the whole revealing tremor hadn't lasted even a minute. He was saying apologetically but coolly, "I'm afraid I wasn't the—warrior type. I had rather a time of it after I got out."

"More men than you'll ever hear about did," Sentry said briefly. "And small wonder."

"Thanks, it's nice to think. But—you know women——" Farrar paused, inviting Sentry to know women. He wasn't bitter, he was sadly tolerant. "They like the ribbons, and any other ornamentation you pick up. But nerves . . ."

That could be it, Sentry thought; you could make a tactful and considerate hell for a man over that, by saying in effect, "Don't even glance at that poor unfortunate, he'll think you're staring." And people would look strainedly in every direction but his; in Farrar's case there would be sudden silences, and avoidance of all service discussion . . .

Or it could be the other way.

Farrar had risen. He said, whole and polished again like a miraculously mended plate, "I shouldn't be talking about nerves to you . . . Good Lord. It must be frightful to think how close you came."

Sentry waited.

Farrar said with a peculiar intentness, "To being killed. You could so easily have been, I understand. Well, in the midst of life and so forth . . . you're sure there's nothing I can do?"

A reply to Sentry's night letter came that evening. It was a straight wire from Phoenix, Arizona. It said, "Re your inquiry Lieutenant Charles Farrar was our guest from March to June of 1945. R. O. MacPherson."

James Court was brisk. Just as Farrar had seemed sympathetically at home in a sickroom, he was restless and uncomfortable in it, his lazy eyes shying away from the bandages, the pills, the bedclothes. He said, coming in, "I heard Charles parted with a bottle of his best, and it seemed like a good time to come and drink your health. How's the head, by the way?"

"Still attached," Sentry said. "Thanks for hauling me in."

Court shrugged, sniffing appreciatively at his brandy. "Glad I was on hand. How are you feeling? Somebody said you'd drawn a blank."

Sentry said that it hadn't been a blank, that it was only an impression that escaped him. "—and maybe not even that. Just because you've never walked into a hole before doesn't mean you can't."

"I suppose not," Court said reflectively. "You did a good bit of swearing and flailing when you began to come to, though. You also shouted for some name of a name to get off you."

"Really? I seem to have heard that's the usual delusion," Sentry said.

Court gave him a slanting glance. "Probably . . . When does the doctor say you'll be up and about? This is certainly no way to spend a vacation."

Palmer had said possibly Thursday; they would take X rays that day and it would depend on what showed up. This was Tuesday noon. "Tomorrow," said Sentry.

Court nodded; his face showed nothing but polite interest. Sentry said carefully, still watching him, "By the way, there's something I meant to ask you before. How about mail in prison camp? Did any get through?"

Court uncrossed his legs, lifted the brandy bottle inquiringly and at Sentry's shake of the head refilled his own glass. "Mail . . . Lord, we'd have given our heads for it on the work details. A lot of people have told me they wrote, and I think some of them did, but we never saw a letter in all that time. But Nick," said Court, eyeing Sentry warily, "had just gotten a bundle through the Red Cross when I reached Cabanatuan. All delayed, you know, and arriving en masse."

Sentry nodded. It was suddenly appalling, the realization that they had all written a last letter to Nick and none of them had known it, Nick least of all. But even if you knew it were a last letter, what would you say? He switched his mind away from that. He said, "Mine among them, I suppose, and Sarah's?"

"Yes, he gave me what news there was from here," Court said. He was lighting a cigarette, his sleek gray head bent, his face preoccupied. "The usual things, not exciting but wonderful to hear when you've heard nothing. Mrs. Trellishaw wasn't well—she's a very sick woman, you know—Jane and Megan were fine, the duck eggs had hatched, they'd repainted the living room, Sarah had gotten a job in New York. Nothing world-shaking, except that a letter from home always is in circumstances like that . . . Why?"

"I just wondered," Sentry said.

And he had. He had wondered how Sands would have found the cold courage to come back into this small closed group of people after what he had done to Eleanora Ware. Sarah's letters answered that. Personal mail would have been easily accessible in a prison camp—and Sands had only to find out that there was, up until this late date, no hue and cry over the man who had been at the wheel of Eleanora's car. No suspicion of murder, of a callousness almost beyond belief . . . as you were, in relation to the Trellishaw family.

Sentry became aware that Court was holding a cigarette end with an inquiring expression. He said absently, "There's a blue thing——" and stopped.

The shallow blue glass bowl with the sliding silver lid that Sentry had vaguely assumed was an ashtray was gone from the small table near the armchair. He had never looked inside it. Miss Tibbett had probably taken it away to wash; she had a habit, which Sentry suspected was intentional, of removing all the ashtrays to the depths of a kitchen cupboard. That was what he thought then; later he wondered how he could have missed what was, looked at with hindsight, a staringly plain declaration of fact.

Court came over to the bed to extinguish his cigarette in the metal tray on the table there. He was polite and a little bored and anxious to be gone. "Well—nice to see you recovered, or nearly. You didn't look very hale on Saturday night, and I can't help feeling, under the circumstances," said Court with his lazy smile, "a rather proprietary interest. You probably want your lunch, so I'll be off . . ."

Sentry lay quiet, counting up his gains. They had all asked him casually or concernedly when he would be up and around again. With all but one of them it would have been the usual polite inquiry; to Sands—if Sentry were right in his persistent feeling that Nick had named his and Eleanora Ware's murderer and Sands had not been able to find and destroy the postcard—it might very possibly mean a deadline.

Deadline. Not from the Latin, but still full of meaning and none of it nice. Sentry pondered his Colt briefly. He picked up his book then and read page twenty-one haltingly, four times, before he fell into an uneasy sleep.

That was on Tuesday afternoon. It was Wednesday morning before Sentry learned that late on the preceding evening Megan Ware, on returning ahead of her family from a lengthy dinner out, had been struck down savagely in her bedroom at the Trellishaw house.

15

IT WAS SARAH who told him about it. She had lost her armor of crispness that morning; without it she looked vague and distracted and strangely subdued.

She said that they had all—she and Jane and Megan and Megan's mother—decided that it was too hot for dinner at home and had gone out to MacFarland's, an old restaurant on the water, for cold lobster and whatever breeze they could find at around eight. Megan had complained of a headache before they left, and halfway through dinner she had abandoned her pretense of eating and asked the waiter to call her a cab. She refused to have anyone drive her home; it was her fault, she insisted, for coming in the first place. She had looked miserable, and said she was going straight to bed.

". . . So naturally we took our time," Sarah said, "and when we did get home at nearly ten the police were there and Megan was in hysterics and the doctor was waiting to take her to the hospital—he wanted her there overnight for observation. She'd hit her head badly, or been hit. Aunt Harriet collapsed in the middle of all this, which made," Sarah was grim, remembering it, "quite a diversion—she has a very shaky heart. And poor Jane——" She stopped.

Sentry's attention had been halted sharply. "Megan called the police, then?"

"No, as a matter of fact it was Miss Glass, Cy Stevenson's aunt. She'd come to return one of Jane's garden books, and when she saw lights and didn't get an answer at the door she went in and found Megan, of course."

"Did Megan say what happened?"

"Only that she'd gone upstairs to her room and someone—she's pretty sure it was a man—opened the door of my room, which is just before hers, and leaped at her. The next thing she knew someone was knocking at the front door and she was still too stunned and frightened to answer it. Luckily it turned out to be Miss Glass, who doesn't stand on ceremony outside doors."

"Your room," Sentry repeated thoughtfully, and Sarah gave him a quick cool glance. "Mine. Sounds rather scarlet for Swannet, doesn't it? As it happens I haven't the faintest notion of why a thief would settle on that one."

A thief. Death, like a thief in the night . . . his deadline had worked. The trap had sprung, and it was empty.

Or—completely empty? Sentry thought not. He looked at Sarah's bent shining head, at the fingers playing nervously with her straw handbag. He said mildly, "Was anything missing?"

"No." Sarah must have been aware of the flatness of that; she smiled suddenly. "Believe me, this is not idle conjecture. Jane called Charles last night, she thought he ought to know, and after Charles had seen Megan settled at the hospital and talked to the doctor he came around to the house. He had us make lists," Sarah said, her eyes widening at the mere recollection of it, "of all the jewelry and things we owned. We were half-dead by that time and having a drink before bed, but we made the lists. Aunt Harriet's, for her and Megan, was quite impressive, but Jane and I showed up very badly. And then we checked, and there was nothing gone at all."

Their eyes met over the issue of Nick's letters, the letters Sarah had said were in the house and now could not be found. "Nothing," Sarah repeated evenly, and stood up abruptly and turned her back.

Sentry said to it, still almost carelessly, "What do you make of it all?"

There was a long moment before Sarah said haltingly, "I—don't know, except that it's rather . . . terrifying. To go into your house in a town like this, where you've always lived, and be sprung at——" She turned then; she looked to Sentry desperate and at the same time withdrawn, like someone asking mercy from an enemy.

She said, "It's possible, isn't it, that there's some sort of vagrant or thief around who attacked both you and Megan? You told Jane there was something you couldn't remember about your being out there on the porch on Saturday night. Mightn't it have been a sound that struck you as suspicious, that—more or less decoyed you out? After all, they're head injuries in both cases . . ."

Sentry stared at her, feeling a sudden pound of blood in his temples, an abrupt deadening of all his alerted senses. She's asking for an out, you fool, he thought savagely; she's as near to being on her knees as you'll ever see her. But it shouldn't have hurt the way it did, as though he were watching some aloof and lonely thing brought into submission. Maybe it was for Nick's sake that he hated to see her standing there humbled and uncertain and asking him to accede to something that her own clear logic must tell her he knew was nonsense.

"It's possible," he said without expression, and then, "When are they letting Megan out of the hospital?"

"This afternoon. It was just shock and a bad bruise on the back of her head," Sarah said, picking up her handbag. "Charles and Aunt Harriet are driving over after lunch to pick her up."

"Do you think you could get Jane to go, too?" Sentry asked it almost absently, his thoughts centered ahead.

Sarah stared. "I suppose so. Why?"

"Because I'd like to come over this afternoon," Sentry said pleasantly. "There's something I'd like to see. What time?"

◈ *155*

"Three," said Sarah, braced in the doorway. "If that would suit you?"

"Nicely," said Sentry.

It was the first morning he had been up; Miss Tibbett had departed after breakfast with the dour hope that he would take care of himself. Sentry stretched himself on the bed and gazed at the ceiling. He wondered whether Megan Ware had gone home the night before because of a headache or because she had arranged to meet someone; he wondered whether she had told the exact truth about what had happened to her when she arrived.

He wondered, not for the first time, about the terms of the will that had placed Jane Trellishaw in her present anomalous position—jailer, or privileged sister?

He wondered how many other people had realized that in the event of Megan Ware's death Sarah Devany was next in line for inheritance.

Megan Ware's bedroom was yellow and white, shadowed by the branches of the apple tree that touched the end window and allowed only a dappled view of the pond and the ducks. The south windows, between folds of linen, looked out on the rock garden and the hill. The room was serene and cool and immaculate, so pointedly so that Sentry turned for a sardonic glance at Sarah, standing silent and furious in the open doorway.

Her chin went up a little. She said icily, "Hadn't you better get started, Andrew? After all, I can't stop you—unless I call the police, and I think everyone had enough of that last night."

Sentry ignored her tone; he said merely, "Thanks, I will," and crossed a yellow rug to the mirror-topped bureau. He was vaguely surprised to feel no qualms at all as he began to pull out drawers and go methodically through their contents. After the first few moments he even stopped being conscious of Sarah's wardress stance in the doorway.

He had come here without much hope of finding Nick's letters; it was too much of a shot in the dark. But Megan Ware's story didn't stand up to even the most casual analysis. She had said her attacker came out of a doorway she had already passed —when he could so easily have waited until she entered her own room and then slipped down the stairs and out of the house. A far more logical conclusion was that by her premature return she had surprised Sands in a search of her room, or another part of the upper house, and had been struck down there in darkness.

These drawers had been tumbled through very recently—by Sands? By Sarah, whose air of cold astonishment might have been assumed to cover the fact that she had guessed what Sentry would want in this house?

The drawers were scrupulously neat at first glance—stockings still in their original slim boxes, gloves in a quilted case, soft folds of white and pink and pale yellow, scalloped or edged with lace. Underneath, in almost every drawer, was complete raked-over confusion. Earrings, a tumble of them caught together. Cigarette lighters, a pair of thin silver bracelets, a thimble, a shoehorn, a letter-opener. Under the nightgowns a mad profusion of small things: hatpins, lipsticks, compacts, wallets —it looked like the accumulation of years.

Someone—Sands?—must have dumped all these things together in a rapid but complete search, hadn't had time to replace them but had covered them instead with a bland surface of order. But still——

Behind Sentry Sarah said in a calm and deadly voice, "You're quite good at this, aren't you, Andrew?"

Sentry didn't answer. He pulled open the bottom drawer and looked at a folded white blanket. He had an odd feeling of incompleteness, as though the room had something more to tell him if he had had the time and knew where to look. He stooped and ran an exploring hand over the smooth light wool. There was a hard object under it. He threw back folds of blanket and with a sense of complete bewilderment, lifted out a shallow blue glass bowl with a silver lid.

Sarah must have noticed his sudden immobility, because she crossed the room quickly and stood at his shoulder, saying in a changed voice, "What is it, Andrew?"

Sentry turned silently, and watched her eyes drop to the bowl he was still holding. Sarah put out her hand with a swift instinctive gesture. "But—that's mine! I did miss it from my room this morning, but what in the world is it doing here?"

"Yours?" Sentry went on watching her, almost sure it was a lie, but baffled by her look of honest puzzlement.

Sarah nodded. "They were a pair—Aunt Jane picked them up at auction and gave one to me and one to Miss Glass. Of course—hers is in the cottage, isn't it? But I can't imagine how this one . . ." Her face cleared. "It must have been the cleaning woman. We had a new one this week and I suppose she couldn't remember where to put it back and stuck it out of sight instead. I'll take it if you don't mind, Andrew—or," said Sarah politely, "had you planned to have it fingerprinted and photographed from several angles?"

At that, and at the accumulation of days of bitterness, Sentry's anger came splashing abruptly to the surface. "Listen," he said coldly, "listen to me. You've stood in my way at every turn ever since I first told you what I'd found out about Nick. You've fed me lies by the spoonful and I've swallowed them down like a good boy—and to hell with that from now on. Now you stand there when your cousin has just been cracked on the head in her own home and tell me I'm straining at gnats."

Sarah took an involuntary step forward. Her face looked very white in the shadowed room. "Wait, Andrew, I——"

"Ah," said Sentry coolly, "this one's going to have sugar on it. Don't bother, Sarah, because I've finished what I wanted to say. Except that I'm not, as you seem to think, playing games to annoy you. I'm looking for a killer, and he was here in this house last night—— My God, why shouldn't he be? He's a true-blue friend of the family."

Sarah put a hand to one temple and drew a long breath, and suddenly, as eerily as though an invisible radio had sprung to life, there were voices.

"—better lie down, even if it's only for a little while."

"But they've had me lying down at the hospital all morning —I don't think I'll ever sleep again."

And then Jane Trellishaw, calm and peacemaking: "Do as your mother says, Megan, it can't hurt and you might as well be on the safe side."

Sarah was rigid with horror; Sentry had only time to think, This bedroom's at the back of the house, this is how Sands was caught, before he took Sarah's wrist and urged her not very gently toward the door. "Quick. And for God's sake answer me——" He raised his voice casually as they came out into the hall. ". . . But this part of the house isn't as old as the rest, is it? The floors are entirely different."

"No, this was an addition . . ." Sarah was creditably calm as they started down the stairs and encountered the startled gazes from below: Megan, Harriet and Jane Trellishaw, Charles Farrar. A little behind them, tactfully withdrawn, was the lounging figure of James Court.

"Oh, you're back," said Sarah too briskly to the blank lifted faces. "How do you feel, Megan, and what did the doctor say . . . ?"

Sentry added his own inquiries, made polite farewells and went out into the steamy gray afternoon. His head ached dismally. He wondered with a certain sour satisfaction, as he drove away, how the imperturbable Sarah was going to get out of that one.

It could never have been a police matter, his search for Sands, and he would not have wanted it even if it had been possible. But there were, Sentry reflected, drawbacks. The whereabouts of all these people last night about eight forty-five, for instance —that might have been instructive. But he knew only that James Court rented a small summer house in Pine Bluff, four miles away; that Charles Farrar had taken a room at an inn somewhere along the harbor, and that Cy Stevenson was staying with his aunt. They were all free agents; Court and Farrar had cars. Cy had only his aunt's, and she had used it to return a book to Jane Trellishaw that evening.

The rest of that day was savagely hot; Sentry went back to the cottage and stood under a cool shower and found that getting dressed again undid the whole business.

Meanwhile, Sarah's innocent surprise at the blue glass bowl in Megan's bureau drawer had resolved itself; she had seen it, of course, in the mirror before he turned, and she had had a moment in which to arm herself. Why had Megan taken it? . . . because the smooth tale of the pair bought at auction was scarcely believable, under the circumstances. Or had it been Megan—or another of his visitors?

Megan was, after all, Eleanora Ware's sister. It was logical, almost inevitable that she would have known more than their cousin or aunt about Eleanora's intimate concerns, and at twenty-two and twenty-four you were apt to be confiding. Had she known something about Eleanora's death all these years, had she been profiting by it? Had Sands perhaps tried to wipe away the proof, and failing that——?

It was no good, any of it, and Sentry threw it overboard with reluctance. Even Megan, who was hard and measuring behind her deliberate naïveté, would hardly make capital of her sister's fate. Besides that, she was amply provided for now and would some day be a very wealthy young woman. You didn't feel a necessity to gild the lily unless——

Well, there was always that.

Sentry made himself a rum old-fashioned, dispensing with the fruit and sugar and bitters, and drank it with a sudden sharp consciousness of the hot black silence outside the windows. Was this a part of Sands' maneuver with the Colt, this awareness of vulnerability? Disarmament by force was always a complete and basic humiliation; you felt the need of weapons twice as strongly after you were left defenseless and waiting for attack.

The waiting seemed all at once intolerable. True, he had forced Sands into one unscheduled move, but how long had he to brace himself for the next? And in the meantime he had been dispossessed of his gun as briskly as a naughty boy of his dollar knife. So that when he did unmask Sands, when he was face to face with the man who had watched Nick crumple and sag under Japanese rifle bullets . . . Sentry looked thoughtfully down at his hands. His wrists felt taut; he watched the tendons relax as though they belonged to somebody else.

For the moment, there was nothing to do but wait. And know that you could build up only so much pressure inside a sealed vessel before the lid went skyrocketing.

Sentry went out to dinner and came back, and found a prepaid telegram under his door. He opened it with delicate fingers, because there was no one now from whom he could logically expect a telegram.

There were the usual codings above the message; after he had read it Sentry went back and deciphered the time of sending: 5:13 p.m. today, from Swannet. Then he read the message itself again, because it was somehow incredible that it should have been set down by brisk impersonal fingers and then sent unmolested on its way to him.

It was very short. It said: SUGGEST YOU DROP RESEARCH AT ONCE. OR WOULD YOU RATHER I SENT SARAH TO JOIN YOUR FRIENDS? I CAN DO THIS IMMEDIATELY AT YOUR DECISION. It was signed, very simply, SANDS.

◇
◇ *16*
◇

THE WESTERN UNION OFFICE occupied a corner of the drugstore
next to a soda fountain where a scattering of young customers
were curved limply over coke and ice cream. Sentry walked
into the bluish-white blare of light, cold still and steady, and
stood before the enclosed counter. A blonde waitress behind
the fountain glanced at him and turned her head to call over
the whir of a malted milk, "Rose!"

Rose emerged from the depths of the prescription department; Sentry could not have said later whether she was dark
or fair or either side of ninety. He knew detachedly that his
errand here was useless but that it had to be performed, and
when she said briskly, "Yes, may I help you?" he pushed the
telegram across the counter.

"I'm a little confused as to who sent this, I didn't think my
friend was in town. I wondered if you'd happen to remember
what he looked like—the man who sent it?"

She was dubious, lifting the telegram. "Not just offhand.
Maybe if I looked at the written form . . ."

There was a pause while she riffled through papers, drew one
out of a sheaf. Then she said concentratedly, "Yes, here it is—
it was a kid, I remember that. Couldn't have been more than
eleven or twelve—he copied it off a paper he had and paid
for it. Sending it for his dad, I guess . . . that help you any?"

Sentry drove bleakly back to the cottage, not disappointed,
because he had expected nothing else, but still full of a quietly
consuming rage. He went the long way, so that it took him

past the Trellishaw house, and idled the motor at the opening in the tall privet hedge. He was rewarded sooner than he had thought to be; in a few minutes a figure came into the small front living room and knelt before the bookcase under the window. There was a momentary gleam of smooth hair under the lamp, and it was Sarah.

There was no reason at all for the relief that washed through him; the telegram had come only forty-five minutes ago. As for the impulse to leave the car and go up and tap on the window and speak to her . . . the heat and his own edged nerves, Sentry thought. Nevertheless, he sat in the darkness and watched her rise and walk into the inner part of the house before he let in the clutch and drove away again.

There was a car parked in front of the cottage, and as Sentry pulled up into the driveway a blackness shifted and rose on the steps, to the left of the headlamps. Sentry was tightly motionless for a second, bent forward over the wheel, his fingers still gripping the hand brake, his muscles gathering. Then Cy said out of the darkness, "Hi, I'd about given you up. Nice invalid you turned out to be—and after I'd brought some cold beer to solace you."

"Good idea." Sentry got out of the car and locked it and followed Cy up the steps. In the doorway of the small kitchen, while Cy thumped a laden paper bag down on the drainboard and took out two cans pearled with cold, Sentry said casually, "As a matter of fact I took a run down to the drugstore."

"Pills again? Where do you hide your beer openers?"

"On that nail over the sink. No, Western Union."

There was a swish of sound as Cy applied the hooked opener. "Glasses, or as is?"

"As is," said Sentry. This was like bouncing a ball at a cushion, he thought; nothing came back at you. But in the living room, with the windows open on the airless night and moths flickering at the screens, Cy repeated, "Western Union. Lord, you're not thinking of going back to town yet, are you?"

Sentry shook his head. He said, "Just—checking," and handed Cy the telegram from Sands.

The instant it left his fingers the possibility of danger struck him; if Cy had sent it he might assume that Sentry's silent confrontation meant knowledge of his identity as Sands. And someone had the Colt, the loaded Colt.

Cy's hand went into his pocket and came out again with cigarettes and Sentry's hands on the chair arms unclenched. Cy said, lifting his eyes slowly from the yellow oblong, "But this is——" and read it incredulously through again. His voice sounded genuinely appalled. "It's an open threat, for God's sake. Just like that. And sent through the office right here in town—what did you find out about it?"

Sentry shrugged, holding out a hand for the telegram. "What you'd expect."

"You mean somebody got hold of a kid and asked him if he wanted to make a buck?"

Sentry nodded without speaking. Cy stared, his face perplexed, a little of his ruddy color gone. He put a match to the cigarette he had forgotten to light and said brusquely, "Well, look here, Andrew, this tears it. I thought this might have been a wild-goose chase of yours, God forgive me, but now you've got something to act on, go to the police with."

"Have I?" Sentry laughed shortly. He didn't need to glance at the pasted lines in order to quote. " 'Research . . . send Sarah to join your friends . . .' How sinister does that sound, unless you know what I know—and happen to believe it?"

He stopped. He said softly, "Besides, it's my own job—and I've been looking forward for some time to the finish."

◆ 165

There was a small pause. Cy said finally, "Okay—but what are you going to do about it?"

"I don't know yet."

"I suppose there's no chance at all that he's—bluffing?"

The terrible and unnecessary loss of Nick, the new defenseless grief on the face of Robert Twining's sister . . . "None," said Sentry.

It seemed to him for the first time a little unreal, this businesslike conjecture over the next move of a murderer, a man who signed himself openly, mockingly, Sands. Sands—it was almost generic now in Sentry's mind, an identification of evil. But outside the summer darkness carried only the serene pulse of water in the cove, the occasional song of a cricket. Sarah Devany would be reading or taking a shower or brushing her hair in the house over and beyond the hill, and Sands was debating whether to kill her or not.

"Well," Cy said heavily into another silence, "if you're going on with this, as I presume you are—— My God, isn't this unbelievable?—Sarah is going to have to be watched. I mean really watched, stayed with. What are you going to do about that?"

Sentry had already thought of one possibility, but only as a last resort. He said again, "I don't know. It can be worked."

Cy drained his beer. He stood up and said awkwardly, "I can help if you want me to. Tomorrow, say, I can hang around pretty much all day—tell them my aunt's been working me to a standstill and I'm on temporary strike. Which isn't far from the truth, by the way. That would leave you free for a little while at least."

Sentry hesitated. Then he said, "Why don't you do that, Cy? It's not going to be long now. I know why Sands had Nick shot, I know why he killed Twining, I know what he's after here— and when I find him I can make it stick."

Cy only nodded thoughtfully at that. At the door he stopped to say that he had been over to the Trellishaws' to inquire about Megan, and what did Sentry make of all that? He said uneasily, "That accident of yours—and now this attack on Megan—it's all connected, isn't it? It can't be coincidence, all this business in a town like Swannet. Even if you can't remember it there must have been something . . . any light on that, by the way?"

Sentry said there wasn't, and Cy shook his head worriedly. He said that Charles Farrar had spent the preceding night at the hospital, that James Court was trying to arrange police protection for the Trellishaw house during the next few nights.

"And not getting anywhere, as far as I know," Cy added. "Well—I'll see you. And for God's sake don't stick your neck out, will you?"

Sentry woke in the night with a faint alarm just beyond the reach of memory. He brought himself up on his elbow to listen, but there was nothing now except the slide and rustle of water in the cove and the usual leafy night sounds. He had been clenching his teeth in his sleep; his jaws still felt tight and strained. Gradually, shreds of a vividly bad dream came back. Sands was in it, and Sarah.

Sands and his hostage. Sands, who had come out of his secure and quiet corner to fight for his life, who would show no more mercy to Sarah than he had shown to Nick or to Robert Twining. What would it be—another accident? Or a bullet through the white forehead, from the convenient Colt .45?

The thought of that drove wakefulness along his every nerve.

Lying in the dark, knowing that any action whatsoever on his part would break the grim deadlock between himself and Sands, Sentry began to wonder for the first time whether it was the letters and his search for them that had driven Sands into the open. After all, Sarah had received and read them and they had obviously looked innocent enough to her. Well, Nick mightn't have learned of Eleanora Ware's death until too late to write back his own knowledge once he had connected the two; letters from home had been known to go astray or arrive fantastically late. And no mail at all had gone out after the fall of Bataan.

Which left the postcard—and Nick couldn't be sure, in spite of his projected escape, whether he or Sands would reach home first. He would want to prevent any future contact between Sands and the Trellishaws, but he wouldn't dare hand Sarah, thousands of miles away, knowledge that might prove fatal to own.

And he wouldn't know who, besides Sarah, would read the postcard.

Still, if there were a clue concealed in the necessarily innocuous message, Sands hadn't had cause to worry about it yet. Then was there something else . . . ?

Sentry went stubbornly back over it again, building around himself a black rainy night and Nick's departure from the last party Eleanora Ware was ever to know. He lay awake a long time, driving his mind against the wall of years.

He had an appointment with Palmer for X rays early the next afternoon; at two o'clock Palmer said with finality, "Well, you got out from under that one, Mr. Sentry. I thought so, but I wanted to make sure. Is it giving you much pain?"

Sentry said it wasn't and Palmer nodded. "Those stitches can come out at the end of the week. You'll have a scar showing, of course, but I notice you have one there already." He made another note, closed a file folder and put it into a wire basket. "What's somebody trying to do—buy your vote the hard way?"

"You might call it that," Sentry said; "Thanks," and walked out into the hot, low-skied afternoon. He felt curiously unhurried as he drove down into the town and stopped briefly at the hardware store. He returned to the cottage and spent an energetic half-hour and then, holding himself back from too much hope, set out in the car for the Trellishaw house.

Farrar met him at the door, his air of confident well-being gone, his eyes haggard. "Come in, Sentry. Glad to see you so well recovered. The others are outside—come on back."

He was obviously abstracted; he looked almost ashen, as though the padded props of his comfortable life had been knocked out from under him. I could look ashen too, Sentry thought callously, if all that money had been nearly on its way to the morgue. But that wouldn't answer, because he would have sworn Farrar's concern was deep and sincere. And besides, the other man had the air and bearing of accustomed financial ease. (*Money in the background, I'd say*—that was Lyons.) "How's Megan?" Sentry asked abruptly.

"The doctor says she'll be as good as new in a couple of days. But my God," Farrar said sharply, "do you think any of them realizes that she might have been killed? I tell you, it's——" He broke off, shaking his head. "And this house, open. Open, mind you, with all the silver and some valuable jewelry and irreplaceable china . . . They're covered, I've seen to that, but still——!"

Lament over a Silver Compote, thought Sentry. He followed Farrar to the door that opened on the terrace and the back lawn. Sarah was there; his eyes found her instantly. She was stretched out on a chaise longue, laughing at something Cy had said; Sentry discovered to himself that it was a long time since he had seen her like that, her head tilted back, her face gay. Cy, on the grass beside her, wore a warm perspiring look. Megan was in a deck chair under the apple tree, her eyes closed. Next to her in another chair Harriet Trellishaw kept an anxious vigil.

Sentry looked around, docketing them. Court was absent, and there was no sign of Jane Trellishaw. Megan opened her eyes as the porch door swung closed and he exchanged politenesses with her and Mrs. Trellishaw. Megan's artless innocence was very much in abeyance today; her eyes had a hunted shadowy look, her mouth was defiant under her mother's almost constant gaze. And wasn't there something a trifle odd in Harriet Trellishaw's steady surveillance—a grimness that jarred with the supposition of natural maternal worry?

Sentry had only a fraction of his attention to give to that. His mind was preoccupied with the one small detail that had slid into his head when he lay awake the night before. It was a very tiny scrap indeed, so routine and matter-of-fact that it would have been omitted from even the most conscientious account of events on the night Eleanora Ware had died. It might mean nothing when he tracked it down except a stupidly tenacious crossing of t's and dotting of i's.

Or it might mean everything.

Because it was probable, almost certain, that the police, the doctor, the first frantic concern over Megan Ware two nights ago would have brought back into all these people's minds that other night, the night they had retired after a party without knowing that Eleanora was bleeding to death on a road in the dark. Sentry's own presence would inevitably remind them of Nick, so that there might have been recollections voiced.

To one of them, Sands, the small query that now raised itself in Sentry's mind might have come as a sudden and unsuspected blow.

Sentry kept his excitement down grimly, because above all

this visit of his must look idle and natural. He greeted Cy and Sarah, and when Farrar had drawn up a deck chair and was deep in conversation with Megan and Harriet Trellishaw a few yards away he said casually, "By the way, is your Aunt Jane around? I'd like to thank her properly for all the aid and comfort she sent while I was a bed patient."

"Jane?" Sarah glanced across the lawn and then up at the rock garden. "She was here a few minutes ago . . ." She lifted her voice. "Does anyone know where Jane is?"

Sentry didn't like that; it came uneasily close to making an issue. He was aware of Cy's sober worried gaze. Then Harriet Trellishaw said indifferently, "Jane's in the house, I think. That new woman is doing the linen closets, and hasn't a notion of where things go. It's very tiresome, I must say. If you have to police someone's every move you might as well do the work yourself."

You mean, thought Sentry, that Jane might as well do it. He stood, still casual. "I'll just call up to her then. I don't want her to think . . ."

"I'll go with you," Sarah said, sounding a little breathless. "I think she wants me to shop before dinner."

So two could play at this game. Sentry held the porch door for Sarah and followed her silently into the house. He wasn't surprised when she turned to face him in the shadowed inner living room. Her head was high, her eyes direct and challenging. She said stiffly, "You can believe this or not as you please, Andrew. I was going to tell you yesterday when the others came. When you came to my apartment that first night and I went to get you Nick's letters they were gone. I thought I could get them back myself without any—unpleasantness, that's why I told you they were up here."

Listening, Sentry wondered if he looked as undecided as he

felt. It might be the truth; it would certainly explain her steady and transparent evasions. On the other hand, sudden changes of heart were always suspect. Watching her, trying to measure her eyes and voice and hesitations, he began to ask questions. She said she had kept Nick's letters, with the postcard sandwiched among them, in a quilted white velvet stocking case, a lavish and useless gift from the Christmas before. She couldn't remember when she was last sure of seeing the case in her bureau; she was positive it wasn't more than a month, possibly less, before the evening Sentry had arrived to ask so urgently for its contents.

Sentry said flatly, "You thought your cousin Megan had removed the case."

Sarah looked away. "I didn't know what to think." She was calm and very steady, but her eyes were suddenly stark. "If you'll remember, I had something else to think about just then."

A small indeterminate sound brought Sentry's head sharply around. He checked his breathing for an instant, and was aware that Sarah had been caught up in his immobility. Then footsteps sounded from the floor above, and Jane Trellishaw's voice said dimly, "I think that's all, Marion, except that Mrs. Trellishaw would like——"

Jane. The only person, in all probability, who had the answer to what he wanted to know.

Sentry turned back to Sarah. He said rapidly, "Go back outside. Stay with the others, with all the others, until I come out again. I've got to talk to Jane, and then I may not need the letters."

He watched her go and listened to the click of her sandals along the porch before he went quickly into the small front living room and up the stairs toward the sound of Jane Trellishaw's voice.

She wasn't startled. She looked shockingly older, that was all, and staring, as though she were being forced to look at something she had deliberately kept out of the range of vision but hadn't forgotten for a moment was there.

She said quietly, sitting on the edge of a candlewick-covered bed opposite Sentry, her hands lifeless in her lap, "I think I knew in the back of my mind, in spite of what the others said. Eleanora was—untrammelled, yes, and she'd been foolish, very foolish, and . . . indiscreet. But she'd never have gone out, even after a party, and picked up a man she didn't know, a stranger. Never . . . I think I always knew," repeated Jane Trellishaw steadily, "that if the man who was driving her car that night could ever have been found, we'd have recognized him as someone she'd gone out with at some time before."

She went on staring dryly at her hands; Sentry kept his vigil at the window. It was a small guest room beside Sarah's at the back of the house, looking out on the lawn and the tilting rock garden. At the top of the hill, motionless as a tree in a poster, a young maple hung leaves of fierce fiery green against the flat sky. By shortening his gaze Sentry could see the top of Sarah's smooth-brushed head and folds of her thin cool dress. Cy was still sprawled on the grass beside her like a large and anxious watchdog. An outcropping of roof under the window showed him nothing of a third figure except a pair of white-clad feet extended on the foot-rest of a deck chair . . . Farrar's? Or Court's? These people never remained separated for very long.

There was no reason for his feeling of impatient hurry, because even if Sands had been goaded to danger point, even if he suspected Sentry's continued sojourn inside the house, nothing could happen to Sarah while she sat in full view among a group on the lawn. Nothing; Sentry knew it with his mind and distrusted it with every instinct. He turned back to Jane Trellishaw and said abruptly, "Nick met this man running away from the accident—I'll tell you how I know that later. Meanwhile I've got to know this: what was Nick wearing when he left the house that night?"

". . . wearing?" She repeated it with a stupefied air, her mind obviously elsewhere.

Sentry leaned forward. He said patiently, "You told me before that the Friday Nick and Sarah arrived here from New York it was hot and sunny—" he waited for her puzzled nod and then went on; "—and that it rained hard all Saturday evening."

"Yes." Jane was still staring, but her concentration had turned inward. Sentry gave her a moment, because the accuracy of her memory was the crux of this whole slowly rising structure. "Did Nick set out to meet his cab that night just as he was—in his uniform? Or," Sentry asked it with careful intentness, "did he borrow a raincoat?"

It couldn't have taken her more than two or three seconds to answer; it seemed longer than that to Sentry because her face was shuttered with recollection and told him nothing. When she said slowly, "Why, yes, he did, an old one of my brother's," he felt a peculiar stillness inside him. He waited. Jane said, "I remember because Nick was a good deal taller than Howard and the coat was so short on him. It was a disgraceful old thing, but it was the one Sarah found first and Nick said it didn't matter, he'd only be wearing it as far as the cab and that he'd——"

She halted. She said in a faintly puzzled voice, "He was going to send it back by the driver. I wonder if that's what . . ." She stopped again.

Sentry said nothing; he was afraid to coax her, afraid that she might manufacture, out of uncertain memory and an anxiety to help, a truth that wasn't there. He hadn't long to wonder. Jane said suddenly, "Of course . . . Amby, the driver, turned up at the house the next morning. There was a policeman there at the time, and we were having to make—arrangements. I remember the maid coming to me with a brown paper package and saying it was something for my brother, and he wasn't there, he was doing something about the funeral services. I never thought about its being the raincoat until now, but of course it must have been."

It was as simple as that. The raincoat, a dubious possibility, a figment of his imagination in the small hours of the night, was all at once a thing of fabric and buttons and fact—and more? Sentry held his exultation back, because the corollary was still to come. Sands might have stopped bleeding by the time he blundered into Nick on the hilltop. Or there might be stains, stains that Sands hadn't realized he had left, that Nick hadn't seen when he took off the raincoat in a darkened cab. A signature in blood . . . Palmer had said there was blood on the handle of Eleanora Ware's car door—and coagulation would hardly have been hastened by a pounding run immediately after the accident.

Sentry said with restraint, "And what did you do with it? The package?"

"I told the maid to take it upstairs, as I remember, to put it somewhere, anywhere. For all I know, it may still be with Howard's things."

Here in the house. Where two nights ago Sands had been rummaging until Megan's arrival had brought his search to a premature end. Sentry said rapidly, "Do you think you could find out, Miss Trellishaw? Without letting anyone know what you're looking for? It may be vital, it——"

He realized at that instant, with the house quiet around them, that moments had passed while he kept his attention riveted on Jane Trellishaw's face and voice. He swung his gaze sharply away and down between folds of curtain. The lawn was serene and burningly green under the leaden sky, and Sarah was not there.

17

SENTRY CURSED HIMSELF instantly and bitterly and was out of the room and down the stairs, brushing past a startled Megan halfway up. His sharp interrogative, "Sarah?" echoed emptily back at him from the cool hollow rooms.

If anything had happened to her . . . his mind took him no farther than that. And it wouldn't happen here, he thought steadyingly, not where it would be so easily traceable later.

But it might happen wherever Sarah had gone.

The porch door opened and James Court came in at an amble. He seemed surprised at the sight of Sentry; he started a greeting and Sentry said, cutting across it without warning, "Where's Sarah?"

Court looked further surprised at the abruptness of Sentry's tone. His eyebrows went up, but he said coolly, "In here, I thought. At least, I didn't see her come out again."

He was evidently looking for something; a moment later he took a package of Harriet Trellishaw's denicotinized cigarettes from the mantel and started for the porch again. He said over his shoulder, "I imagine she's upstairs," and was gone.

But she wasn't upstairs, because he would have heard her and there had been nothing but the descending footsteps of the cleaning woman. Sentry made a rapid search of the first floor, trying to tell himself that Sarah could have absented herself for any number of safe and innocent reasons. But if she had come into the house and had not been seen to emerge and was nevertheless not here, it could only mean that she had left the house by another door. Deliberately, because she hadn't wanted to be observed. Sentry was at the front door and through it, and then he was running.

The duck pond, secret and dark behind its protective wall of trees. Not deep, but deep enough, and conveniently accessible from the front lawn if you wanted to go there without being seen. Sentry pushed past the screening branches, his breath harsh in his throat, and stopped short. Sarah stood in profile a few yards away, watching the white weaving progress of the three ducks. She lifted her head and turned quickly as the branches swished into place behind Sentry. She said expectantly, "Well?"

The calm inquiry of that struck Sentry momentarily speechless. He knew that he had panicked over nothing, that he had reacted exactly as Sands had known he would, but that it would take a few minutes for word to get around to his still unevenly pounding heart. While Sarah stood there and looked, incredibly, a little impatient. He said controlledly, "Will you tell me what in the name of God you're doing here?"

Sarah took a step toward him. She had seemed astonished at first, but now she was cold and extremely angry. "Until just now, I was waiting for you—or possibly the message you gave the cleaning woman for me slipped your mind. You do forget yourself quite often, don't you, Andrew?"

She was walking furiously past him; Sentry caught her wrist. He said, "Let's have that again, slowly," and Sarah hesitated and then told him. Sentry listened and admired the simplicity of it in the middle of a spreading coldness.

A few minutes after Sarah had returned to the lawn the cleaning woman, Marion, had emerged from the back door and had conveyed by a series of winks and nods that she wanted to speak to Sarah. "I thought it was about my room, or maybe something she'd broken and was worried about," Sarah said. "But of course it was that you would meet me at the duck pond right away, and not to let anyone see me if I could help it." She paused, uncertain for the first time. "You did, didn't you? Leave her the note?"

"No," said Sentry watching her face. "She must have—confused the names. Did she show you the note?"

Sarah shook her head. "She'd mislaid it, or at any rate she couldn't find it, so she came out to tell me anyway."

Sentry pushed his own warning thoughts back. He said cheerfully, "She saw me going upstairs to talk to Jane. She probably only half-read the note somebody left her and automatically assumed it was from me. She didn't look like much of a deep thinker. And as nobody came to meet you, she obviously got the whole thing backwards."

Sarah looked relieved but still a little doubtful. As well she might, thought Sentry. Because this had been—what? A trial run? Or, more probably, Sands' way of warning Sentry that his bluff was not to be called? Pasted words on a telegraph blank: 'Shall I send Sarah to join your friends? I can do this immediately at your decision.'

And he could, he had proved it. Sentry had thought to surround Sarah with an unconscious but automatically protective cordon, and Sands had lifted her out of it, had isolated her neatly and easily with no more trouble than a note, promptly destroyed, left for a strange servant.

All right, Sentry thought coldly. All right.

But it would take engineering.

Sarah made a small movement and they both looked down at her still imprisoned wrist. Sentry took his hand away casually and Sarah rubbed the wrist lightly. She said as though she had just remembered, "What did you really want to see Jane about, Andrew?"

Careful; now, of all times, she must know nothing, so that Sands, watching for conspiracy in a glance, a gesture, an inflection, could not find it. The violence had crept out to the end of its chain, and the slightest suspicion would send it leaping.

"To thank her," Sentry said in a tone of surprise. "You wouldn't believe the number of poached eggs I ate before she came to the rescue. Which reminds me, I still have a very fine collection of the Trellishaw china over at the cottage. I don't know what Farrar would say."

Sarah didn't smile. She turned a little away, her face remote. "I thought it might be something about—that you might have found——"

"It's getting late, if you have shopping to do," Sentry said firmly. "I'll drive you, I have a few things to pick up myself. Shall we go consult Jane? . . ."

The town was idle and nearly deserted; not odd, Sentry thought, when every street on the harbor side showed a brimming blue cup of water at its end. The heat was steady and savage, with the taut quality that precedes thunder. Colors were deeper, distances distorted in the hot still gray light; the twisting streets, the old housefronts, the occasional vivid thrust of a small shop's canopy all had an operetta air. Sarah, glancing wistfully down a side street as Sentry drove through the town, said, "We'll be back in time for a swim, won't we?"

"Oh yes," Sentry said easily. "We have the place to ourselves. Here? . . . Right."

Sarah disappeared into what seemed to be a combined stocking shop and rental library between dotted-swiss curtains. Sentry, reconnoitring, found a small ice cream parlor nearly opposite. There was a public phone booth at the back that afforded, between posters, a wedge-shaped view of the street leading away from the stocking shop and toward Sentry's car. Sentry sandwiched himself into the booth, just ahead of a large determined woman in a black-feathered hat, and dialled.

The woman later told her bored son-in-law that it had all been most extraordinary; that the man in the booth had inquired for someone in a distinctly odd voice and had then said rapidly, "Sentry. But I'm your grocery order or the hardware man when you answer me. It's a quarter to five now. When the phone rings at five-thirty . . ."

At that point the black plumes of the listening woman's hat had dipped too close to the glass and she had moved haughtily away. But not, she said, before it was perfectly plain that there was something peculiar about that man's phone call. Just the offensive way he looked at her showed he was up to something . . .

Sentry emerged damply from the booth and went out onto the street. He knew he was skating on very thin ice indeed, and he was not at all sure that this elaborate series of phone calls would come off. It had to; it was as bare and simple as that. If he had had more time . . . but, after six slow and empty years, there was suddenly no time beyond the next few hours.

Sarah was waiting in the car. Sentry said, "Where to?" and Sarah said, "Lemons and bitters and I'm through. What about you?"

"Putty and cigarettes," said Sentry briskly. "Not as drinkable as yours. Meet you at the car again?"

He didn't want putty but he bought it anyway and, for verisimilitude, a small putty knife. Hardware stores were places you could linger while making sober and hardheaded selections, and this one was no exception. The proprietor was bored and lonely among his deserted counters, and went lengthily into brands, qualities and the high cost of puttying. At twenty-five after five Sentry concluded his purchases and went out to the car to say, "Sorry, that guy was interminable. I'll pick up some cigarettes and be right with you."

There was a phone booth in the stationery store, and no one outside it this time.

He found out later that the afternoon had proceeded, at the Trellishaw house, exactly as he had hoped—but then Jane, who knew the house and its inmates and its guests, would not have dared to make her murmured and hasty suggestion just before Sentry had left in his car with Sarah unless she were sure of the vacation routine.

He learned that James Court's suggestion of their all dining out together had been instantly welcomed; that Cy had at first refused and then allowed himself to be persuaded. That they had sat around the long living room with all the windows open having a languid early cocktail, without the bitters Sarah was to bring, when the phone had rung and Jane came away from it to say, "Poor Sarah. She couldn't say much, of course, but she met Jenny McCampbell in town—you remember Jenny, Megan —and she dragged her off to meet her fiancé. Sarah said she wouldn't be roped in for dinner, but knowing Jenny I wouldn't be too sure . . ."

They had lingered over their cocktails, turning on lights against the strangely early dark. Harriet Trellishaw said indifferently that she would have to do something about the dinner she owed the McCampbells; Charles said weren't they the people who had bought the old Trevor place? Megan, cross with the heat and piqued at the general disappointment over Sarah's absence, remarked that Jenny McCampbell had been fortunate to get herself engaged at all, no matter to whom. At close to seven o'clock James Court said, "Look, is this hopeless? Can't we extricate Sarah? Family crisis, or farewell evening, or something? It is pretty close to the end of vacation at that. Who will bell the cat?"

"I never heard of the McCampbells. I'm out," Cy Stevenson said comfortably.

Jane was shaking her head at James. "Don't look at me, I won't be trapped by Mary McCampbell. It's either you or Charles—you've both met her but she can't in all conscience keep you talking for hours, even about her daughter. Tell her," said Jane, unexpectedly callous, "that Harriet isn't feeling well —but don't, for heaven's sake, alarm Sarah."

In the end it was decided that Court should do it. There was a wait, too tight to only one of them, while the receiver drawled. Then Court said, "Mrs. McCampbell? . . . James Court. You probably don't remember me, but I——" There was an interval while he described the health of the Trellishaws and inquired after that of the McCampbells. After a decent pause he said, "I'm actually calling for Mrs. Trellishaw—I don't know whether Sarah forgot that she'd planned a dinner of sorts. Vacation seems to be the only time that we can all . . . oh, I see. No, it's nothing formal, it's just that we didn't know whether or not to wait. Thanks very much . . ."

He said, returning to the living room, "She's gone out to dinner with them. Damnation—but it can't be helped. Are we off? . . ."

In the cottage, Sarah stood straight and still and furious, facing Sentry across the little living room. She said incredulously, "But you can't keep me here. You can't even intend to try."

"Don't be a fool, of course I can," Sentry said shortly.

He was tired and on edge and his head hurt with a regular

pulse-timed pain that was like another separate enemy. He knew he had put his point baldly and too flatly, that he had thrown it at Sarah almost like a challenge; but how in hell, he asked himself wearily, did you break it diplomatically to a girl that you were going to kidnap her for a time? A girl whose hostility was like a second skin?

Sarah watched him steadily. She said, "They'll come looking for me, you know."

"Not for quite a while. You see," said Sentry, "they have it on good authority that you're somewhere else." At the small flicker of fear across her face he felt an odd bitter anger. "My God, Sarah, hasn't all this penetrated yet? I told you I'd just handed the telegram to Jane when I went haring out of the house after you this afternoon, and that I didn't have a chance to get it back. Would you have believed that, if you'd seen it? Of course," said Sentry, "I might have sent it myself, let's not overlook that—but you won't have, I'm sure."

Sarah didn't answer him directly, she said instead, "Jane knows, then."

"Yes, but Jane won't tell. Not even," Sentry said, "your very good friend Mr. Court."

She was silent, considering that, trying not to let him see the visible crumbling of her strongest defense. Sentry said, knowing it for what it was, the willful probing of an old injury, "Why haven't you married Court, Sarah? Your way was clear a long time ago, and you weren't standing on ceremony even before that, as I recall. Where's the lawful impediment?" He shook his head. He said, "Somebody's hanging back."

Sarah still hadn't moved. She took his words without any outward sign beyond a faint warning pink high on her cheekbones and a tiny backward tilting of her head. She said curiously, "You don't really want to know, do you, Andrew? But I'll tell you. I don't know why I bother, except possibly to prick that barrage balloon you've carried around for so many years."

The anger was raw between them now, burning away the newer, surface animosities, blanking out Sentry's urgency. He had an odd notion that this, whatever it was, was not going to matter nearly as much as he had once thought it would; beyond that he felt nothing at all.

Sarah said, "James came to my cocktail party that day to give me the message Nick had sent. I'd gotten Nick's card the day before. I was so happy I didn't know what to do with myself, except maybe see a lot of people and froth over at the edges. It's hard to keep that kind of thing to yourself, much harder than——"

She stopped short, her eyes bitter. After a moment she went on, still in the same level recitative voice, "It wasn't the first cocktail party that day for James. He was celebrating his own homecoming, I was part of a background he'd known for years, and when he took me aside to deliver Nick's message he got— affectionate. Apart from the fact of his being an old friend, it's not quite the thing for the hostess to scream for help in her bedroom. And at that point," said Sarah quietly and precisely, "you walked in, and you drew exactly the conclusions you wanted to draw. You have no margin for error, have you, Andrew? Ever?"

Sentry found his voice with an effort; he had been, in a twinkling, as unbalanced as a man who had stepped firmly and solidly onto a log which was a crocodile instead. He said the only thing there was to be said out of the knowledge that this was the truth and that he had been bitterly and humiliatingly wrong.

"You could have told me. Or stopped me, without a word. If you'd only . . ."

But it was too little and it was six years too late. Sarah gave him a long and unflickering glance and then turned her face away, and Sentry knew he had been answered. He was still standing motionless, trying to find a footing where there suddenly was none, when she said simply, "Well, that's that. We've misunderstood each other nicely, haven't we, Andrew? I'll go quietly now, but I'd like a drink—didn't you say you were going to have one before you left?"

Sentry seized on that; it was temporary ground, but it would do. He said too briskly, "Good," and started for the kitchen. "Sarah, I don't know how to——"

She had been waiting and watching and playing for that one split-second of grace. She was across the room and wrenching at the lock, had the door open on darkness before Sentry caught her arms and then, easily, her wrists. He pushed the door shut with one shoulder. He was unprepared for the swift violent jerk with which she partially freed herself; he recaptured the frantically reaching hand and pulled her toward him, close. He said, laughing, "Strong, aren't you?"

Sarah stared furiously back at him, her breathing still rapid, her face pale. She said, "Let me go, Andrew," and then, almost whispering it, "Let me go."

"Yes," Sentry said slowly. "Yes, I'd better."

He dropped her wrists abruptly and watched her walk warily away from him toward the fireplace. He thought bitterly that he should never try approaching this girl with anger because it would always, treacherously, turn into something else. His contempt at his own weakness made him savage; he said shortly, "All right, Sarah, upstairs. Or would you like to be carried?"

Sarah whirled and mounted the stairs ahead of him, her back a challenge. At the head of the steep narrow flight Sentry went past her and opened the planked door and struck a match to light a candle on the bureau just inside. The slant-ceilinged room quivered halfway up out of the shadows: twin beds, a small straight-backed chair placed against the chimney enclosure, three little windows on either side and one at the farther end. The windows were shuttered and fastened from the outside.

Sarah's eyes went instantly to the empty light socket and then to the single chair. She said stonily, "Aren't you going to tie me up?"

"And have my will with you? Not just now," Sentry said. "I have more pressing duties elsewhere. There are cheese and crackers over on that table if you get hungry. You'll find another candle in the bureau drawer. I shouldn't be long."

He went to the door and closed it behind him and bolted it; the metal made an angry clanging sound. He said to the planks, "There's a bolt on your side too, if you get nervous," descended the stairs, turned off all the lights and locked the cottage securely behind him. There was no reason at all for the fear that outstayed all precautions; he told himself that when, with the car backed into the road, he looked up at the cottage. It was completely dark, a self-effacing part of the night around it. And Sands had no business here; Sands' objective was, Sentry was grimly sure of it, the same as his own.

He knew at the same time that his reasoning, his plan, the strain that had increased and tightened all through the long hot afternoon hung by an extremely slender thread. Yet wouldn't Sands' strength necessarily have lain in the very slenderness of the thread? Now that someone else knew of the thread's existence, Sands would move quickly to cut it. So quickly, perhaps, that his easy smiling identity would slip and Sentry would be able to look, feature by feature, at the face of the man who had murdered Nick.

There was no moon. A few slow heavy raindrops struck and

glittered against the windshield as Sentry drove slowly past the Trellishaw house. The blaze of lights startled him until he realized that after the occurrence of three nights ago, when Megan had surprised an intruder there, they wouldn't want to leave the house obviously empty.

Sentry passed the Trellishaw driveway and drove another two hundred yards. There was a house for sale set back from the road behind a wild tumble of weeds and saplings; he had noticed a grass-grown driveway that afternoon. He put his car well into thicker blackness under trees and walked back to the Trellishaw house.

The rain made soft puncturing sounds in the maples. Sentry caught himself standing rigid, staring over his shoulder at the black line of the hedge and the paler opening in it. The living room lights lay in warped oblongs on the wet grass, deepening the shadows where they stopped. Sentry circled to the right and went around toward the back of the house; Jane had said she would leave the porch door unlocked. It was very black here; a dew-wet branch of wild cherry slapped without warning against his forehead. Sentry smothered an instinctive sound and went on.

The porch door opened quietly—as though it mattered, Sentry reminded himself irritably, in an empty house. But it was always hard to convince yourself that a house was empty, particularly when there was lamplight shining softly on polished tables, when there were ashtrays and matches waiting for use, when there were so many empty doorways for someone, anyone, to enter suddenly.

Old Shell-shock Sentry, thought Sentry caustically, and went briskly around to the staircase and up.

They didn't, thank God, have one of those attic openings in the ceiling that required chairs and then acrobatics. There was a doorway and stairs—next to the linen closet, Jane had said. Sentry unlatched a door, looked in at stacked sheets and towels and opened the one beside it. Stairs stretching up and away, blackness like a cave at the top; Sentry waited an instant, listening. Then he took his flashlight from his pocket and switched it on, closing the door behind him.

He wasn't surprised at the neatness of boxes and barrels and corded books; any attic under Jane Trellishaw's thumb would automatically be a well-conducted one, in which you would actually be able to find things. Sentry located the tall green metal filing case at once, back against a wall. He crossed to it, his footsteps sounding loud enough in his own ears to reach the street, put his flashlight down on a wardrobe trunk and glanced at his watch. It said seven forty-five, but it had said seven forty-five when he parked the car. Sentry swore briefly to himself and turned his attention to the filing cabinet.

"In the top drawer, under some envelopes," Jane had said. "I can't be sure, of course, because it was such a long time ago and I didn't give it more than a glance at the time. But as I remember it, it looks like the package Amby brought to the door that morning."

Sentry reached under manila envelopes discolored with age and lifted the package out. The brown wrapping paper, the tough kind used in post offices, was stiff and dusty under his fingers. The contents were soft. Sentry hooked the cord that bound it over a corner of the open drawer and pulled, and the cord snapped. A corner of the wrapping crackled and rose sharply, and he was looking at what, at the last minute, he had hardly dared to expect after all—a fold of tan gabardine.

A bundled-up raincoat.

The coat Nick had worn when he left this house on a summer night almost exactly nine years ago. It had been raining then, as it was raining now, filling the attic with a hollow drone. For an instant Sentry's whole existence shrank to the radius of a flashlight's glow, was concentrated into the small circle of buttery light that held a dust-filmed filing cabinet, a forgotten package, his own momentarily rigid hands.

But it still mightn't be——

The hell it mightn't, Sentry thought, abruptly and savagely certain, and tore the wrapping paper back with a lacerating crescendo of noise. He found the shoulders of the raincoat and shook it as free as the folds of nine years would permit and stared in sudden flat quiet at the crumpled right sleeve. There were dark smears halfway between the cuff and the elbow, stiffened into the heavy fabric. Bloodstains, preserved almost as well as though they were last week's, because they had been protected from air by layers of folded-over cloth and thick paper and the confines of a file drawer. Sands' blood.

There were witnesses to the fact that Nick had worn this raincoat on the night Eleanora Ware had died. Nick's own blood type, Sentry knew, had been O-negative and comparatively rare. On the strength of the coat and the times involved it would certainly be possible to get tests made, to have——

Sentry pivoted, but not quite quickly enough. He had dropped the raincoat instinctively; his outflung hand went instantly to the flashlight. Turned off, it became a weapon of sorts, was at least not a beacon to point him out. He braced himself for the lunge that was gathering in darkness, but the plummeting contact caught him on the shoulder and spun him violently to one side. He dove forward again and closed for an instant with the vicious strength and the throat-seeking hands. Laboriously, in darkness echoing with rain and the sound of heavy breathing, he began to fight for his life.

◆ 190

18

IT DIDN'T LAST LONG. The flashlight had been knocked from
Sentry's grasp and he used his hands with a kind of savage
pleasure. He touched metal once and knew it was the Colt, and
then it came down on his healing temple with a burst of white
light. The pain was a blotting, absorbing thing, like a bandage
across his eyes, across his very consciousness. Before the dizzi-
ness had rocked away the attic light sprang on, pale and harsh
after the darkness.

For a last second or two Sands' anonymity clung; he was still
a shape and a faceless presence. Then Sentry's vision cleared,
and he looked squarely across the lighted space.

And this was Sands.

He had never had to fight with one of his victims before, and
it didn't become him. He was swaying a little from reaction, his
face wet and chalk-white except for a red bruise with a rip of
blood along the center on one cheekbone, where Sentry's
knuckles had opened it. His hair was tumbled on his forehead,
and the smiling mouth had already begun to swell. He no longer
looked like a junior banker, but he still looked pleased.

He said between laboring breaths, "That was quite an ex-
hibition, Mr. Sentry."

"My strength is as the strength of ten," Sentry said light-
headedly, "you bastard."

Farrar moved the Colt a little. His hand was steady, but the
knuckles flexed and the fingers shifted, as though he were finding a grip that suited him. Not a man who liked or was used to

the balance of a gun, which explained why Sentry had not been shot from the stairs. And which made him that much more dangerous. He could hardly miss at five feet—or could he? While that was going through Sentry's mind Farrar's smile broadened.

"Don't try it, Mr. Sentry. I'm by no means an expert shot— but I can guarantee at this distance to get you between the eyes, or at least in one of the eyes."

"Are we waiting for something?" Sentry asked steadily. A bullet was a good deal less dangerous, with a man like Farrar, when you were moving. If he watched that restless finger, if he didn't allow his glance to so much as flicker up to the eyes that were so incongruously filled with venom . . .

"Yes, we are," Farrar said pleasantly. "We are waiting to find out who else knows—who else you told—about this raincoat." He stirred it with his foot, not moving his eyes from Sentry's face. "Take your time, Mr. Sentry. Smoke a cigarette if you like. I want you to remember accurately."

Very slowly, Sentry took cigarettes from his pocket and lighted one. He mocked at his own involuntarily listening stance—Farrar had undoubtedly evolved a logical reason for leaving the others and he himself had made a prisoner of Sarah. But he could still wait—for Farrar to suffer a heart attack, for lightning to set the house on fire, for even, humiliatingly, the sharp satisfying taste of what stood a chance of being his last cigarette.

Farrar was eyeing him curiously. He held the gun almost too unwaveringly, as though he were having to give it more of his attention than he liked. He said, "Why didn't you let it alone, Mr. Sentry? You couldn't get your brother back and the net result was the same, to you, as if he'd been, say, killed in action. When Sarah told me I was surprised, I must say, about our talkative friend Church—because that's who you met. Church is a bigamist—not his fault, a deception on the part of wife number one, as I understand it, but still the law isn't apt to be so tolerant." He shook his head a fraction. "It's too bad all around that you didn't let it ride."

Let it ride, Sentry thought incredulously. He raised his eyes for an instant from the mouth of the gun and stared hard at what appeared to be the other man's sober puzzlement. The color was returning gradually to Farrar's damp white face; he had brushed the hair back from his forehead and touched his handkerchief to the raw red spot on his cheek. A wash, a shave, a bit of gauze, a judicious touch of cologne and he would be, Sentry realized wonderingly, as good as new—inside and out.

The moment for answering him directly was gone. Sentry said, measuring the distance between them for the tenth time, "The way what you did to Eleanora Ware was let ride, you mean."

Farrar was instantly, shockingly furious; the Colt swung up sharply until it pointed straight at Sentry's face. It lowered gradually, and Farrar, his forehead shining, said almost casually, "Come now, it's hardly the same thing. After all, someone might have arrived on the scene in time—those just happened to be the breaks. You've done research on Eleanora, haven't you, Mr. Sentry? Did you find out that she was a very foolish girl? Not that I wasn't foolish too. It would have been much better," Farrar was reflective, looking coolly somewhere inside himself at the faces of Eleanora and Nick Sentry and Robert Twining, "if I'd stuck to my muttons with Megan. But Eleanora was hard to handle, very. Gay, you know, and the devil with the consequences. And worth it, too, really."

Sentry felt sick; he flattened his cigarette between his fingers and realized as he did so that it was over half-consumed. Farrar

◈ 193

saw the gesture. He said sharply, "All right, let's get it over with. Who have you told about this raincoat?"

"And what will that get me?" Sentry asked it evenly, wondering if it would be three or five or ten seconds or as much as a minute, wondering if he could keep braced and ready that long or if his muscles would betray him into passing the exactly right point.

"It won't get you anything at all," Farrar said frankly. "Not a thing. But it will keep me from taking steps against the wrong people, which you might possibly care about—though in your position I can't say I'd be too concerned myself." He took a deliberate half-step forward with no change of expression at all. Sentry said, "Wait."

"Oh, I can wait," said Farrar, "but not too long. It wouldn't fit. Imagine my horror and consternation, Mr. Sentry, when I came back for Megan's pills and found you here—rummaging through the attic, armed and apparently out of your mind. We struggled, of course," he raised an ironic hand to the cut on his cheek, "and I managed to get hold of your gun, which went off while we fought over it. Guns do—it's one of the many things," said Farrar with distaste, "that I've never liked about them. And one of the reasons why we're talking now—I couldn't afford to have bullets sprayed all over the attic. But don't mistake me, I can handle this one. Well? . . . You told Sarah about the raincoat, didn't you?"

"No!" Sentry knew he must have shouted it, because the echoes came rushing back at him above the steady swish of the rain. The blood seemed to drain away from his head and hands and heart at the sound of Sarah's name in Farrar's quiet speculative voice. He calmed then; he said bitterly, "What good is this going to do? You won't believe me anyway."

"Oh, I believe you so far," Farrar said briskly. "You're just chivalrous enough not to have confided such a foolish thing in Sarah. Well, then? Not Megan, I don't think you quite trust Megan."

The rain had brought wind with it; a shutter thumped somewhere. Sentry heard it, Farrar heard it with the faintest wary flicker of his eyes. Sentry said, "No. And not only because she's a kleptomaniac."

"Poor girl," Farrar said mildly, "I didn't know you knew that, they've always hushed it up. I found it out, of course, it was why she broke our engagement before I went overseas. She was visiting my family and there was a small disturbance over some earrings of my aunt's—not too valuable but irreplaceable sentimentally. Someone," said Farrar, showing his teeth, "was ill-advised enough to mention his suspicions, whereupon Megan got very stiff and haughty indeed—separating me from some eventual three hundred thousand dollars. At that price you can afford to overlook certain little quirks of your wife's; in fact you find they're contagious. Well, not Megan anyway . . . Jane? Dear good busybody Jane, who acted as though she'd owned Eleanora body and soul?"

Sentry couldn't answer; he was wet and cold, knowing detachedly that this was much more terrible than he had thought. The slow sensible process of elimination, the death sentence, because it would be that, with Farrar, passed on someone in this low-ceilinged room with the hollow pound of the rain as a sort of ghastly background music. There was a chance that he would live to remember this indelible thing. But there was a better chance that he would not, and it was a frightful decision to have to make, the deliberate throwing of a life in Farrar's deadly path or the blanket silence which might, in afterthought, seem to indicate Sarah.

Cy . . . that crossed his mind with a nightmare quickness.

Cy was better able to protect himself than Jane, than Sarah——

Farrar said with satisfaction, "We've hit it, haven't we? Jane would remember what had become of this coat, Jane was the only one that could really help you—and you'd have sworn her to secrecy, wouldn't you, just for protection's sake? Jane has allergies, you know, some of them quite dangerous. Wasp stings with her have the same effect that tetanus——"

He broke off sharply. In another world a voice, soft, desperate, deafening to them both, said, "Operator . . . operator!"

The Colt flickered up and the white tight finger went back and Sentry, his timing gone wild, was headlong in a flat racing dive. It was almost like close artillery fire, when you went where you had to go with only your last-minute disbelief that you could actually be killed this time as a shield, and there was that same moment of not knowing at once, in the confusion of blood and nerves and muscles, whether you had been hit or not.

Farrar spun backward and over the edge of the stairs while the attic still echoed with the roar of the Colt; it went off again, wildly, at the height of his backward plunge. Sentry picked himself up dazedly and followed, flattening himself against the wall. Farrar, crouched in a heap of shadow at the foot of the stairs, put out a lightning hand for the gun lying on the second step.

"No," said Sentry, and put his foot on the reaching fingers and picked up the Colt. Farrar cried out wincingly and Sentry moved, feeling with the shift of weight a wet stinging throb in his left shoulder near the base of his neck. He said, "Get up."

Farrar stood, groggily. The door to the second-floor hall was open and light struck glisteningly along the whites of his earnestly raised eyes. He still had a remnant of coolness. He said, "Listen to me, Sentry. I won't fight a manslaughter charge in both cases. Otherwise there isn't a thing you can bring against me, you know that."

Sentry looked at the gun in his hand; his wrists and fingers felt curiously tight. He said with an effort, "Downstairs," and Farrar took a step out into the full light of the hall and stopped again. The voice below them said, "Yes, that's it, and hurry."

Farrar went to the top of the stairs with Sentry silent behind him; he put a foot down and turned his head to say uncertainly, "What are you going to do with that gun?"

"I don't know," Sentry said grimly, "but I'm making up my mind. Need some help getting down, Mr. Sands?"

Farrar went. He was still oddly calm, as though in his lawyer's mind he had found an out. Sentry followed him, looking down at Sarah's lifted face where she stood backed tightly against the front door, watching them. He should have been surprised, but he wasn't; it seemed the most natural thing in the world that she should be waiting there.

He saw her as Nick must always have seen her, a little tentative, a little afraid of being hurt again under her air of crisp assurance. With something in her eyes that she was very slow to give and never took back, with a kind of withdrawn beauty that had to be warmed before it could open out. And this with her shining hair tumbled and her face chalky, her palms blackened and her dress dust-streaked.

There was a wordless second when they might have gone to each other, but Farrar was there and the memory of death. Sarah said between pale lips, "I've called the police. I heard the end of it. You're hurt, Andrew, you're bleeding, you——"

"Scratched," Sentry said. "Take the gun, will you? I won't need it, so you don't have to watch if you'd rather not."

Sarah took the gun, and in the transfer their fingers touched briefly. She said steadily, "I don't mind watching at all."

"Just a minute," said Farrar.

He had retreated to the open doorway of the living room,

and his coolness had finally deserted him. He was, as Sentry had first seen him, an image in soap, but without tinting now. He had only a desperate earnestness left, and a foolish parody of his confident voice. He said, "Assault, with a weapon—you'd better not touch me, Sentry."

"Touch you?" Sentry laughed. "I ought to shoot you in both legs and finish you off in the morning. As it happens, I don't want to do it that way."

He walked slowly toward Farrar, toward Sands. He had lived for two weeks in an intimate loathing of this man, and he had not had to ask himself more than once what would happen when they encountered each other. Oddly, half sickly, he found pleasure in examining closely what had been only a shadow before—the dark eyes with the sparks of hazel around the iris, the pores that shone and bubbled with sweat, the neat close ears, the puffed and nearly bloodless mouth.

This was the fleshly shape of Sands, the man who had murdered Nick; this was the thing Nick had bought with his life. Sentry put a hand on Farrar's shoulder and brought him gently and deliberately close. He heard Sarah's sharp indrawn breath and then her stubborn silence; he heard the bitter savage pound of his own blood and dropped his hands suddenly.

"Oh, my God," he said wearily. "If I touched you I'd kill you."

There were headlights then, and doors slamming and brisk hurrying footsteps on the path.

The house seemed very quiet after the police had left. They were sending a doctor for Sentry's shoulder. They took Farrar with them, and the raincoat wrapped carefully; Farrar was charged temporarily with assault and illegal possession of a weapon. The wraiths of official machinery had already begun to take shape; there would be immediate contacts with the army and the Chicago police.

But at the moment there was only the flat empty aftermath, the prickle of rain against the windows, Sarah's face that was only a whitish blur unless he made a deliberate and stabbing effort to focus.

The police car departed. Sentry lifted his head and said, bringing his mind back out of emptiness, "You make a very effective rescue party, Sarah. If you'd lost a minute somewhere along the line . . . How did you get out?"

"The carpenter," Sarah said, and gave him a shaky half-smile. "Yes, really. It seems that Cy's aunt called him about a month ago to do something about the leaky windows in the cottage, and he was busy and forgot all about it until after the storm we had. He was full of compunction and apologies when I finally got his attention by banging my shoe against the shutters. I don't know whether he'll ever come back; he thought the whole thing was very odd."

Her face changed. "Andrew, I found something upstairs there, in the drawer of the bureau——" She stopped, the look of shock coming back to her face. "I don't suppose it matters now."

"What?"

"Nick's postcard, and the letters," Sarah answered slowly. "I suddenly realized where they might be. I'd combed Megan's room pretty thoroughly myself as soon as I got here, of course, because——"

"Yes," Sentry said gently into the silence.

Sarah glanced away. The understanding that he knew about Megan's psychopathic weakness, the thing Sarah herself had tried so stubbornly to hide from him, flickered between them. Then she said, "There was a card of gray knitting wool in the bureau at the cottage, only it wasn't a card inside, it was a folded-over paper with instructions for socks. And I thought——"

Sentry groped foggily for what she thought, and Sarah stood. She said, "Don't come up. Your shoulder——"

"It doesn't hurt," Sentry said.

It didn't, beyond a stinging throb. His head was the enemy, aching as though there were a bellows inside it. He followed Sarah silently up the stairs and into Megan's room, wondering where the moment of closeness had gone.

Sarah turned on the bedside lamp and went straight to Megan's bureau and pulled out one drawer and then another, her hands quick and sure. She took a flat ivory box from under a pile of slips and opened it, her fingers lifting the shadowy folds of nylon inside. She said a little breathlessly, "I don't know where the stocking case is, but that's where she must have gotten the idea. Look."

The stockings were new and unworn, still in their original folds. But there wasn't the usual single sheet of paper inside each pair to separate the delicate cobweb layers. There was, instead, a letter, and under more nylon another letter—the two Nick had managed to get out of Bataan by submarine. In the bottom pair was an oblong of stiff yellowish paper with Sarah's name and address typed on one side—the last postcard from Cabanatuan.

Rain washing at the windows between skirts of striped linen, lamplight blurring the yellow and white bedroom into gold; Sentry stared down at the postcard without speaking.

The top part of the message side was like the one Nick had sent his father, with a check to indicate out of choices that he was "well." The ten typed words said, "Shocked about Noa. Remember our last dinner date. All love." There was the familiar toppling signature in fading ink above the formally-typed full name.

Sentry read it again with a feeling of incredulity, aware of Sarah's flat silence at his shoulder. He said, "But this . . . this——"

"I know. There wasn't anything after all. I thought I'd have remembered if there had been," Sarah said, her voice dragging, "but I wasn't sure."

Sentry thought. He said stubbornly, "What's this about Noa?"

"Noa was Eleanora Ware's baby name. I must have mentioned it to Nick at some time or other. My letter telling him about the crash must have gone astray and never reached him, because this was the first time he'd said anything about it." Sarah's voice was halting and absent. She stared at Sentry out of widened eyes.

"I never thought of it before, but of course that first letter was never mailed. Or at least . . . I gave it to Megan to put with some of hers, and I was anxious about it and asked her later whether she'd gotten them all off and she said yes, that Charles had taken care of it."

So Nick hadn't known, until word reached him from Jane—Court? Sentry looked back at the postcard. 'Noa'—it had a jarring sound of long intimacy. He said, "He'd only met Eleanora once, hadn't he?"

"Yes, over that week-end. I suppose he used Noa because he wanted to save space . . . do you think?"

She was puzzled at his intentness, and Sentry, still holding the unrewarding message in the lamplit room, knew that she had been right in the first place, that it shouldn't matter now. But it did matter in a sense; these were the last words that Nick had said to any of them, and it was ironic that they should have meant so little.

In any case, it wasn't syllables you hoarded on a prisoner-of-war card, it was words. And there was no question mark after what would logically be an inquiry: "Remember our last dinner date?" A Japanese had typed it, of course, with disregard for such trifles as punctuation . . .

A memory stirred in Sentry's brain: Pavick, in the little New York apartment, saying, "Sands snuggled up to the Japs right from the beginning . . . they even had him helping out in the office sometimes."

If Farrar had worked in the office, if Nick had known there was even a chance of his card coming up before Farrar, he would have had to code whatever he wanted to say about the man who had caused Eleanora Ware's death. Would have had to bury it in something just as trivial, just as innocuous as——

Sentry drew his breath sharply. He said, "Your last dinner date. Where was that, Sarah? In New York?"

"Yes." Sarah frowned a little. "It was on Thursday night, because we took the Clipper up here on Friday. We went to Charles', Nick loved their martinis, and then we——" She stopped short, her eyes wide and appalled. She repeated in a dazed half-whisper, "*Charles.*'"

It was there, it had been there all the time if you were looking for it. But Sarah hadn't been and Nick, knowing what he knew, could not have realized that Eleanora Ware's death was a closed issue with her family. Sentry handed the postcard back to Sarah and she put it on top of the letters and then, without taking her eyes from Sentry's, tore them slowly across, twice. She was still standing motionless with the pieces in her fingers when the doorbell rang.

It was the doctor, a small round worried-looking man with rain speckled darkly on his gray hat. He said, "Let's see—a shoulder wound, wasn't it? Well, let's go upstairs and get that shirt off."

◆ 202

"It isn't so much my shoulder," Sentry said, and heard it come out in a mumble. He clung to the newel post, but the stairs went on pitching under his rubbery legs. He said clearly and carefully through a sudden cold sweat, "Wait a minute, I'm going to pass out," and did.

At close to ten-thirty it was Jane Trellishaw who came up to the guest room where the doctor had insisted that Sentry spend the night. It seemed to him days and not hours since he had last been in this room with Jane, when she had sat looking gray and shaken on the end of the bed and he had glanced out of the window to find Sarah gone.

The delayed thunderstorm had begun at last; between the first muttering echoes of it Sentry had heard footsteps on the stairs and in the hall, going past his door, and then the soft final closing of another door and after that silence. Jane, coming in now, said helplessly, "Megan. She won't have anyone near her, but I suppose it's best just at first. Poor child . . . and yet she really seemed able to take it in before the rest of us. I suppose she must have guessed something long ago about Eleanora and —Charles."

And yet, thought Sentry, the poor child had in a way precipitated matters. He said so, mildly, and Jane nodded. She said, "I began to worry, of course, when Sarah phoned me the night Megan came up here from New York. All she said was that Megan had—taken something somebody else might want, and to try and keep an eye on her. I had no idea that it was anything like this, of course, but I did speak to Harriet—her mother's always been able to do more with Megan than anyone else. And then Harriet began to worry, for fear," said Jane ironically, "that Charles might find out. You see, we all thought, and the doctors told us, that if Megan were married and steadied down . . . It never occurred to us that Charles was already ten steps ahead of us. Sarah told me when she called that night that her apartment had just been searched, and I suppose it was he who——"

Sentry nodded. He said, looking at a blue throb of lightning at the windows, "I can't understand why Megan did what she did with the letters after she got the stocking case she wanted—or rather why she didn't do anything with them at all."

Jane stood up. She said slowly, "I know—or I can guess. Megan's always resented Sarah, from the first moment Sarah came to live with us. It's a form of jealousy, I suppose. She didn't know Charles wanted the letters, but she knew Sarah did. That's reason enough for her to have hidden them, I've seen her do the same kind of thing a hundred times. You think it's mischief in a child, but it turns out to be malice in an adult."

Sentry saw that she hated telling him this, that she was forcing herself to say it out of a bitter honesty. Jane went to the door and paused there. She said, "Howard—my brother—knew all this. And about that—other quirk of Megan's. She'd been sent home from two finishing schools, and then when she broke her engagement to Charles just before his commission came through, we all guessed what had happened at his family's. Howard was worried about what might happen eventually, and I suppose he couldn't completely trust Harriet where her own daughter was concerned. That was why he wanted me to stay here with them."

She opened the door. She said quietly, "I haven't done awfully well, have I?" and closed it gently behind her.

Sentry turned off the bedside lamp and lay thinking in what was darkness one instant and flickering luminous light the next. Rain rushed steadily at the windows, the held-back torrent that the heat had brewed. The thunder was close now; it came with a thin hollow crackle and then a shuddering roar, as though it were centered directly over the house.

The doctor had dressed the wound on his shoulder where the bullet had torn in and then out; he had looked at the swollen angry spot on Sentry's temple where there were still stitches, explored it gently with his fingers, and said finally that they would have to wait for signs of fresh concussion.

Maybe this was a sign, Sentry thought, this feeling of emptiness where there should have been exultation because the man who had caused Nick's execution would face execution himself, with longer to dwell on it. But there was nothing at all. Even his hatred had drained away, and he felt flat and lost without it.

He tried to make himself concentrate; they would not try Charles Farrar in connection with Eleanora Ware or Nicholas Sentry, but for the murder of Robert Twining. That would probably take a while, it would mean the unearthing of a clerk in the airlines office or a plane stewardess with a memory for faces, or a bartender in Chicago who might have overheard two men reminiscing about a Japanese prison camp.

That would take care of itself in time; so would the misty gap between Farrar's arrival in the Philippines and the day when he had turned up at Cabanatuan. As for the sudden pallor and dampness, the air of nightmare memory that had overtaken Farrar in the cottage when the question of jeep accidents had come up—had that been a reminder of his initial crime or of something in his war history that wouldn't bear looking at?

And there was MacPherson's, the rest home in Arizona. As far as that went, an ex-prisoner of war could spend his ninety-day recuperation leave anywhere he pleased. The interval would have given Farrar time to patch his nerves together; it would also substantiate his story of having been invalided home . . .

There was another lazy sharp-edged echo and then a deafening clap as the thunder hovered. The door of the guest room opened in the silence after that. Sentry turned his head a little and saw Sarah silhouetted against the light in the hall. He closed his eyes again, feeling a foolish quickening of his pulse and knowing all at once what the emptiness had been, and that he had better learn to live with it.

Sarah came up to the bed so cautiously that only his new awareness told him when she stood directly over him. There was a long moment of silence while he forced his breathing to stay calm and steady, and then her hand was gently on his hair and against his cheek, as tentatively and warily as though she had never touched a man's face before.

Sentry felt the emptiness go with a sudden leap. He put up a hand and caught her wrist and held it there. He said unevenly, "Got you, Sarah—or have I?"

"Yes," said Sarah after a second. Her voice sounded shaky. "Yes. Don't," she said rapidly as Sentry's other hand went out. "Not the light, I mean."

"I wasn't going to turn on the light," Sentry said, "I was just calling up reinforcements."

"Oh—your shoulder," Sarah said, embarrassed.

Sentry smiled in the darkness, lifting himself on his right arm. "Come here," he said, "and give me a hand, can't you?"

He kissed her, and wondered dazedly if it could ever be quite that way again for them both, and kissed her again and it was the same. He had no trouble at all finding her mouth in the dark. When Sarah drew away and said in a soft astonished voice, "Andrew," he said, "Oh Lord, haven't we been a pair of fools?"

"Yes," said Sarah; she had found his hand and was holding it tightly. "Particularly when I knew——"

"Knew!" said Sentry, running raggedly back in his mind.

◆ 206

"That if it hadn't been Nick it would have been you," Sarah said steadily. "I always knew that, that was why it hurt so when you—but you know."

Sentry was suddenly still and flat; he knew she had felt it from the way her fingers tightened on his. There was a moment of indecision when he thought, Ignore it and it will go away, and then he knew he had to ask it and have an answer.

He said, "Sarah, tell me and I'll understand, but tell me the truth for both our sakes. If—all this is because of Nick, because I'm like Nick in a lot of ways, we ought to——"

"Stop that," said Sarah fiercely, "and don't ever say it or think it again, Andrew. I wouldn't have you be Nick even if you could. That was one thing and I loved it but it's over, that was what I was trying to tell you in Megan's room when I tore up the letters. Anyway," she said, sounding as though it came through a smile, "you're a very different kettle of fish, you know, but my own. If you'll have me, that is."

"Have you?" Sentry said violently. "Have you!"

He lay quiet, feeling complete and at peace for the first time in six years, watching intently through the blackness. Presently a flash of lightning rewarded him with what he had been needing to see for the last few minutes: Sarah's eyes waiting warmly and steadily for his under the tilting brows.

Seconds later she said out of the dark, a little breathlessly, "Well, now, look——"

"You're the one who wanted the light off," said Sentry.